# DARK REVENGE:

## *THE TREY TAYLOR STORY*

## *BY*

## *DIANA CARTER*

# DARK REVENGE:

## *THE TREY TAYLOR STORY*

# *DIANA CARTER*

Let's Do This Publishing

P.O. Box 300795
Drayton Plaines, MI 48330
ldtpllc@gmail.com

## OTHER BOOKS WRITTEN BY DIANA CARTER

### BROKEN PROMISES SERIES

*Broken Promises: Shattered Dreams (Republished 2019)*
*When Shattered Dreams Become Reality (Republished 2019)*
*Shattered Dreams The Final Chapter (Republished 2019)*
*In The Name of Justice: The Erica Blackstone Chronicles*

### DARK REVENGE SERIES

*The Trey Taylor Story (Republished 2019)*
*When Time Runs Out: Tara's Quest for Vengeance*
*TJ The Forgotten Brother*

### The Sister Factor Series

*Diamond's Fight for Justice*
*Dior's Darlings Daycare*
*Kristina's Kozy Korner*
*Krystal's House of Secrets*
*Never a Dull Moment: The Nick Jr. Story*

### Single Titles

*The Candidate: The Race to the Top*
*Unbreakable: When Two Hearts Become One*
*The Making of a Legend: Neek's Rise to Fame*
*Unbreakable Deux*

## Dedication

God as the driving force and inspiration in my life has blessed me with the creativity to write yet another book to add to my collection. As I move forward in my writing career, my passion continues to take fold. The **Broken Promises** series rich characters portrayed strength and determination to turn the impossible to the possible. *The Sister Factor* series was more realistic, but the characters with their own unique experiences persisted to get through the tough times while enjoying the good times. A special dedication to Michael Allen McKinney for showing me it's okay to trust again after your world has been shattered into a million pieces.

.

## Acknowledgements

To everyone that has read the **Broken Promises** series, I hope you enjoyed the rich characters. The author's second series **The Sister Factor** promises to be just as enjoyable with characters that will make you think about the everyday world we live in today. As a change of pace **Dark Revenge: The Trey Taylor Story** is different than the family drama of the first two series. This book is a murder mystery about a cop turned private investigator that was framed for the murder of his ex-girlfriend. Watch out for the exciting twists and turns Trey has to endure to clear his name.

I would like to acknowledge a special group of people I've recently met that are a part of my new work family: Robert Clancy, Matt Wasko, Bethany Schultz, Glenda Cruz, Tracy Nadeau, and Emily Marsden. It's been a pleasure working with you guys. Thanks for making me feel a part of your work family. Special thanks to Elaine Jones. From the first day we met you've welcome me into a place that was different but special. Your smile brought sunshine to the entire place. It's my greatest wish that readers that read the **Broken Promises** and **The Sister Factor** series will enjoy **Dark Revenge: The Trey Taylor Story**.

God Blessings,


Diana Carter

## Chapter One

Responding to the call regarding gunfire in the affluent west side area was something Chief Carl Bryson Marshall wasn't looking forward to dealing with in his present state of mind. Normally he wouldn't have made a run like this, but his staff was spread so thin he had to step in wherever he was needed. The outside of the condo was dark and undisturbed, but the door was slightly ajar. Slowly pushing the door open and instructing the two plain clothes detectives to stand on alert, the Captain knocked and announced his name, while pushing the door open further. Not noticing anything out of place in the living room he and the detectives moved slowly into the adjoining room where the scene was totally different.

On the floor in the dining room was the bodies of a male and female. Chief Marshall knew from the disposition of the female body and the two gaping holes in the front of her head that the female was dead. The male body didn't show any physical wounds or injuries, but the gun in his hand gave every indication that he was responsible for the fatal wounds to the female. Upon closer inspection of the bodies the Chief was dismayed that he knew both the victims. The female was none other than his goddaughter, Sonya Elaine Young and the male was the pain in the ass, Trey Adrian Taylor (an ex-cop that resigned from his unit nearly six years ago).

The Chief instructed his detectives to look around and seal all entrances except the front door. Going over to the bodies careful not to contaminate the scene, he went over to see if Trey had a pulse. Discovering that he was still alive he called EMS. Not knowing exactly what happened, but certain he was finally able to do something about all the hell this bum had put his goddaughter through, the chief knew he had to begin to make the calls to the families. He didn't know how to tell his best friends that their baby girl was dead. He also didn't want to call the judge to let him know about his son. He had known Judge Trenton Alec Taylor and his wife Tanya for years. They were nice people that raised their five children well (except for Trey). Trey was nothing more than a spoil self-centered brat. Even though Trey was smart and edgy, he liked to take the law into his own hands. He would have been an asset to the force if he learned to listen and follow rules.

The Chief knew he had to ride to the hospital with Trey once the EMS arrived, so he called forensics. Hearing the sirens as the EMS approached, the Chief went to the door to explain the situation. The coroner was called to take care of Sonya's body. While the techs were working on Trey, the Chief made the dreaded call to his best friend to let him know about his daughter. Holding his breath, Carl dialed Christopher Lester Young's phone number.

"Hi, Carl. How the hell are you doing on this cool and blessed day?"

"Hey, Chris. Sorry this isn't a social call. I have bad news to tell you." The Chief could barely control his emotions.

"Okay. I'm listening."

"Man, I'm at this condo on the upper west side. I received a call about gunfire. When I arrived, I found Sonya, she's dead, Chris." The Chief wondered if the call disconnected because there was no response on the other end.

"Are you there, Chris?"

"You're telling me my baby girl is dead?" What the hell happened to her?"

"We're in the early stages of the investigation so that's all I can tell you right now. I have to go, but I will call you with more details as soon as I can."

"Stop talking to me in riddles man and tell me what the hell happened to my baby girl."

"You know that's all I can tell you right now, Chris. You will be the first call I make when more details become available."

"Talk to you later." Chris disconnected the phone in shock. He didn't know how he was going to tell his wife their only child was gone forever.

8

By the time the EMS arrived with Trey at the hospital most of Trey's family was there. The Chief was sad when he had to call the judge with the news about Trey. He couldn't go into any details, so he just told the judge that Trey had been hurt and taken to Northwestern Memorial Hospital. The Chief found Trey's parents, sisters, his brother Trevor, and his best friend Jerome in the emergency waiting room. The Chief knew he should have called Trey's wife, Malinda Paige Roberts-Taylor first as the next of kin, but decided it was best the judge make that decision since Malinda was fragile dealing with a high-risk pregnancy.

"How's my son doing, Carl?" The judge didn't waste any time with pleasant words.

"I'm not sure, Trenton. He was unconscious on the ride over so we're going to have to wait until he's examined." The Chief knew the judge would have a thousand questions most of which he wasn't able to answer.

"Why did you ride in the ambulance with him? What's going on, Carl?"

"All I can tell you Trenton is that Trey was found unconscious at a house on the upper west side with a gun in his hand, lying next to the dead body of Sonya Young." The Chief watched as the blood drained from the judge's face.

"I don't know what the hell is going on here, but I know you're not accusing my son of murder?"

"All the facts haven't been gathered yet, but that's what seems to be the case. I suggest you call an attorney because when Trey wakes up he'll be arrested for Sonya's murder."

"We have nothing further to talk about, Carl." The judge turned and walked away from Chief Marshall and returned to his family.

"Trent, what have you found out about. Trey?" Trey's mother, Tanya asked her husband.

"Honey, Trey was still unconscious when they brought him in, so we have to wait until he's examined to find out what's wrong."

"We have to find out what's wrong with him soon. We still have to call Malinda." Tanya was head nurse at the hospital and could have found out what was going on before her husband.

"I know honey, but we need to have something to report first. I need all of you to listen to what I'm about to tell you without interrupting me. Carl rode to the hospital with Trey. It seems he answered a call about gunfire in the upper west side area. When he arrived at the scene, he found Trey lying on the floor with a gun in his hand and Sonya lying next to him dead." Trenton had to catch his wife before she hit the floor. It hurt him to the core to see the pain in her face before she passed out. The rest of the family went to the sofa that was on the other side of the waiting room where Trenton laid Tanya down.

"What's wrong with Chief Marshall? Has he been smoking crack or something? There's no way Trey done anything physical to hurt that psycho woman." Tara the youngest in the Taylor family was always in awe of Trey and thought he could do no wrong.

"Tara is right. There's no way my brother would kill that stupid woman even though she probably deserved it." Trevor knew his brother should have done something long ago to get Sonya out of his life, but how could you stop someone as sick as Sonya was from stalking you.

"We have to wait for the details. Please stay with your mom. I have to contact an attorney because Carl said once Trey regains consciousness he will be arrested for Sonya's murder."

"Dad, Linda needs to know what's going on so I'm going over there to tell her. I know mom may not agree, but she's his wife and she has been doing better over the last few weeks." Talia the older of the two sisters was close to Trey's wife, Malinda (Linda for short).

"You may be right baby. You and Tara go get Malinda and bring her to the hospital. Don't give her any details. Just tell her Trey's been hurt and he's being examined." Trenton said.

"Sorry, Dad. I'm not going anywhere until I see my brother." The ever-defiant Tara always had a way about herself. She spoke whatever was on her mind. Even as a small child Trey was the only one able to keep her in line.

"I'll go with Lia, sir." This was the first time Jerome spoke since they reached the hospital. Trey was like a brother to him and he would do anything for his best friend.

"Fine, Trevor, you and Tara stay with your mom while we take care of the rest." Trenton, Talia, and Jerome left the hospital while Trevor and Tara stayed behind with their mom and wondered how they were going to get Trey out of this mess.

## Chapter Two

Chief Marshall sat at his desk the afternoon of the murder. He still hadn't gotten back with Chris yet because he felt bad for both families. Deep inside he knew he had a soft spot for Trey even though he quit the force and took his goddaughter through the ringer. He had to face the fact that on more than one occasion Trey reported the harassment he was receiving from Sonya. He loved his goddaughter, but she was missing a screw when it came to Trey. She was so obsessed with him he had a restraining order out on her, but that didn't deter her from contacting Trey and his wife. Carl had a talk with Chris and Sonya about her behavior to no avail.

Going over the evidence he collected so far, Carl knew he had to get back to the hospital soon. He had to face the fact that it seemed like someone was trying to frame Trey. He had his problems with Trey when he was on the force and thought his family spoiled him rotten, but he knew Trey wasn't a cold-blooded murderer. Convincing Chris was another matter. Carl was there from the beginning, end, and the stalking of Trey and Sonya's relationship. It started years ago, but when Trey was fed up with her psycho actions, he filed a restraining order against her about four years ago. He had to keep renewing the order because of Sonya's unstable behavior.

Both families were in a world of pain which would only get worse. Carl felt stuck in the middle. He wasn't as close to the judge and his family as he was with Chris and Sharon, but he knew the judge and his family were good hard-working people. After the shock when he and his officers arrived at the scene, Carl studied the crime scene. The position of Trey's body was bothering him. He wasn't lying in the position to have discharged the weapon that killed Sonya. Carl made sure he took pictures of both bodies and the surrounding areas of the scene. He didn't think he would never get the look on Sonya's face out of his mind. He felt Chris and Sharon would go for a memorial service instead of a funeral since the wounds to Sonya's head were so disturbing.

Before he headed back to the hospital, Carl was going to meet Chris and Sonya's mother Sharon at the morgue to identify her body. The coroner finally released the body and sent it over to the morgue. He told Chris to give him a call when he was ready, so he could take them over there. He tried to convince Chris not to bring Sharon, but Chris told him that she insisted on being there. He prepared Chris and Sharon as best he could, but he knew they were going to be devastated when they saw the remains of their daughter.

On his way over to pick up his friends (once Chris text him), Carl decided he was going to have to tell them about Trey's involvement. It would be in the media in no time seeing that the judge and his family always seemed to get media attention whether it was good or bad. When Chris and Sharon were seated comfortably in his car, Carl decided to get the dreaded conversation started.

"Guys, I hate that this situation has come to this, but we just have to keep our heads on straight."

"What the hell happened to my baby girl, Carl? You were supposed to get back to me with the details. I've been looking at news programs, but nothing has been said about what happened to Sonya." Chris yelled.

"I'll tell you what I can, Chris. When I arrived at the scene I found Sonya in the dining room of the condo lying on the floor next to Trey." Carl knew Chris was going to go ballistic.

"What the hell are you talking about, Carl? You mean to tell me that punk ass bum murdered my baby girl? I'm going to kill him with my bare hands."

"Calm down, Chris. We don't have all the facts so let's hear what Carl has to say about what happened." Sharon didn't like the way this was working out. This was going to further Chris's hatred for Trey.

"That's basically all I can say right now other than the fact that Trey was still unconscious when I left the hospital."

"You're going to have to do better than that, Carl. I need to know if that no-good bastard was responsible for what happened to my baby girl."

"I can't answer that for sure, Chris. What I can promise you is that I'll put my best men on the case. I'll also personally work on the case to bring whoever responsible for Sonya's death to justice." Carl didn't get to say anything else because they had pulled up to the morgue's parking lot.

When Talia and Jerome arrived at Trey's house, they knocked on the door. They were saddened because the happy look on Malinda's face would soon be gone once she found out what happened to Trey. Talia decided to take her dad's advice and not give Linda too much information before they returned to the hospital. Malinda wanted them to come in and have a seat thinking this was a social call. Then it suddenly hit her, she knew it couldn't have been a social call because Jerome had never come to their house unless Trey was there.

"Lia is something wrong?" Everyone in the family shortened Talia's name except for her parents.

"Linda, I don't want you to get upset, but I need you to come with us to the hospital, Trey's been hurt." Talia's heart was broken to see the scared look on Melinda's face.

"What happened to him, Lia? How could you let something happen to my husband, Jerome? What kind of best friend are you?" Malinda yelled at Jerome.

"Linda, I need you to calm down. Mom, Trevor, and Tara are at the hospital with Trey now so let's join them. We don't have much else to tell you right now." Talia and Jerome followed Malinda as she grabbed her purse and a sweater. Jerome drove so Talia sat in the front seat and Malinda in the back. Talia put off answering any more of Malinda's questions. She knew her sister-in-law was going to lose it when she finds out how much trouble Trey was facing. As Jerome pulled into the hospital emergency area, he let Talia and Malinda out at the car. Finding Tanya, Trevor, and Tara in the waiting room, Malinda went straight to her mother-in-law to ask about Trey's condition.

"Ms. Tanya have you heard any news about Trey's condition?"

"No baby, we're still waiting for an update." Tanya said as she gave her daughter-in-law a hug.

"I don't mean to be rude, Ms. Tanya, but isn't there someone on staff you can push to see what's going on with, Trey?" Linda asked.

"Linda, Trey is with the best doctors on staff. They will come out to let us know how he's doing as soon as they have something to report." As soon as Tanya finished that sentence the doctor and two nurses came out to talk to them.

"Hi Head Nurse Taylor. Sorry it's taken so long to come out to talk to you. After examining your son, it seems he's suffering the effects of being drugged with GHB and a concussion due to blows to the head. He's hasn't regained consciousness yet. As you know the longer, he's unconscious the greater the chance of him coming out of this with his memory in tack is uncertain."

"Dr. Sanders, this is Trey's wife, Malinda. As you can see she's in her last trimester of a high-risk pregnancy. When will she be able to see Trey?" Tanya glanced at Tara out of the corner of her eye and saw she had an 'I know she didn't' look on her face.

"Mrs. Taylor, you can see your husband as soon as he's moved into a room. I ask that he only has two visitors at a time."

"Thank you, Dr. Sanders." Malinda was happy that she would get to see her husband soon. She hoped his mom would go in with her instead of his bratty baby sister, Tara.

"I've contacted Chief Marshall to give him an update." Dr. Sanders left with the two nurses, but not before both nurses gave Tanya and Talia a brief compassionate hug.

"Why would Dr. Sanders contact the police about Trey?" Malinda didn't know what was going on but didn't like the family keeping her in the dark.

"Malinda let's go to my office, so we can talk in private." Tanya asked the nurse at the nurse's station to call her when Trey was moved to his room, then they went to Tanya's office to inform Malinda of Trey's circumstances.

## Chapter Three

Trenton sat in the office the next morning of Victoria Leah Hamilton. Victoria was the best criminal attorney in the state. He used to be amazed at how well she handled herself in the courtroom when he was a presiding judge. He'd seen her pull off some impossible cases and felt she would be able to get Trey out of the bogus charges he was facing. She didn't come cheap, but that's was to be expected from an attorney of her caliper. Listening to her ending her call then instructing her assistant to hold all her calls, Victoria gave Trenton her undivided attention.

"Judge Taylor, I'm so sorry I couldn't squeeze you in yesterday. I was tied up in court all day."

"No problem, Ms. Hamilton, I remember facing you many times in court. I know you have a busy schedule."

"Please call me, Victoria. How can I assist you, Judge Taylor?"

"Sure, and you can call me Trenton because if you take my son's case we're going to be spending a lot of time together."

"What kind of case, Trenton?" Victoria asked.

"Well, it hasn't hit the media yet, but I'm sure in a day or two it will be the talk of the town. My youngest son, Trey is being framed for murdering his ex-girlfriend."

Victoria couldn't believe her ears. She used Trey's services and remembered him when he was a gusty cop. "Oh my God, that's awful. I've used your son's services many times. This would be the last thing I expected to hear about him."

"Well, as it stands now he's still unconscious from being drugged and blows to the head. Chief Marshall said once he regains consciousness he will be charged with murdering Sonya."

"What evidence do they have, Trenton?'

17

"I'll be honest with you, Victoria it looks bad for Trey. He was found unconscious next to Sonya's dead body with the murder weapon in his hand."

"Wow, that is bad, Trenton. I would be happy to take Trey's case Trenton. We can get started immediately. The first step is to arrange an appointment with Chief Marshall. I'll be in touch with you as soon as I can. We'll have to interview your family too. I'm sorry about what your family is going through. After I've touched base with Chief Marshall, I'll come to the hospital to check on Trey."

"Thank you for your time, Victoria. I better get back to the hospital; my wife and youngest daughter aren't taking this very well. Not to mention Trey's wife is in her last trimester of a high-risk pregnancy."

"Your family has their hands full. Don't worry, Trenton we'll get to the bottom of this mess." Victoria walked Trenton to the door and went back to her desk to get started on Trey's case.

Malinda was sitting next to Trey's bed wondering when he was going wake up. She had been up most of the night. God bless her mother-in-law and Talia for arranging a cot to be brought into Trey's room. She still couldn't believe that her husband was going to be arrested for murder once he wakes up. As Tanya and the rest of the family explained the facts of the case to her yesterday, she sat there with tears slowly rolling down her face. She tried to warn Trey many times how psycho Sonya had become and so had his family members. He couldn't explain to Malinda in a way that made sense to her why he didn't completely let go of that crazy woman. Talia explained Trey's relationship with Sonya was toxic. It seemed neither of them was willing or able to give up on each other. Malinda felt Trey had finally let go of Sonya, until this happened.

It didn't help Malinda had to deal with Tara. No matter what Trey did or didn't do Tara was always one hundred percent on his side. The way she looked at Malinda yesterday when her mother was explaining Trey's situation gave her the chills. Malinda tried to understand that Tara was still young and immature, but she felt threatened by Tara staring at her like this was her fault. Malinda was also disappointment that TJ hadn't come to check on his brother. She realized there was tension between the men, but with the situation at hand she thought TJ would be mature enough to leave their grudges behind. What was even more shocking was that Malinda was hearing rumors that TJ wanted to prosecute Trey's case. Malinda's thoughts were put on hold when the most beautiful woman Malinda has ever seen walked through the door. She had a pleasant smile on her face that immediately had Malinda dropping her guard.

"Hi, my name is Victoria Hamilton. You must be Trey's wife, Malinda? Trenton hired me to represent your husband." Taking a close look at Malinda she was surprised by Trey's choice for a wife. Unless she was mistaken it seemed like Malinda was too soft to deal with someone like Trey.

"Yes, I'm Malinda. It's so good to meet you, Mrs. Hamilton."

"That's Ms. Hamilton but please call me, Victoria. May I call you Malinda?"

"Ok, Victoria, you can call me, Linda."

"Trey has done some work for me in the past. I was shocked when his dad told me about his situation. That girl was a nutcase."

"So, you knew Sonya?"

"I only saw her in passing a few times, but Trey told me on many occasions about her obsessive behavior. I was so relieved when he took out that restraining order on her, for all the good it did."

"Just how well do you know my husband, Victoria?" Malinda didn't like how familiar Victoria seemed to be with Trey.

"If you're asking if we have or had a physical relationship the answer is no."

"Sorry if I'm being a little paranoid. I thought Sonya was out of our lives for good until this happened. Are you going to be able to get Trey off?"

Trey heard the voices, but they seemed so far away. It bothered him to hear the stress in his wife's voice. The other voice sounded familiar, but he couldn't place it. His mouth was dry, and his head hurt so bad it felt like it was spinning. He slowly opened his eyes, but the women were so deep in their conversation they didn't seem to notice. Clearing his throat, Trey finally got their attention.

"Oh my God. Trey, I'm so glad you're awake. Let me go get Dr. Sanders." Malinda was beside herself with joy.

"Wait a second, Linda. Let's talk to Trey for a minute." Victoria wanted to prep Trey for what was about to happen. He would've been cuffed to the bed if it wasn't for his mom and sister Talia. Their connections to the hospital gave Trey a brief relief from what was going to happen later today. It also helped that his dad was a former judge with many connections.

"Trey how are you feeling baby?" Malinda realized Victoria was concerned about Dr. Sanders contacting Chief Marshall now that Trey was awake. It saddens her to know that handcuffs would be slapped on Trey sometime today.

"My head hurts like hell. What happened? Why am I in the hospital?" Before Malinda could answer Victoria spoke up.

"Trey, I know all of this is confusing right now, but I need you to listen to me."

"What are you doing here, Tori?" Trey was the only person that called Victoria out of her name. He told her when they first met that Victoria was too stuffy. She suggested Vicky, but Trey told her that name didn't fit. Trey or Victoria didn't notice the strange look on Malinda's face because she felt uncomfortable with the way Trey said Victoria's name.

"Trey what's the last thing you remember?" Victoria wanted to gage Trey's state of mind.

"I don't know. My head hurts, and everything seems to be a blank."

"You were drugged and hit over the head. Linda can you go get Dr. Sanders please?" Victoria wanted a few minutes alone with Trey.

Trey had a strange look on his face when Malinda opened the door and he saw a uniform cop standing on the outside. "Tori why is there a cop stationed outside my door?" Trey was getting upset and the monitors started to beep.

"Trey calm down. Your dad hired me to defend you. Sonya is dead and they're going to arrest you for her murder. You know the drill. Don't talk to anyone about what happened without me being present." Victoria had to get straight to the point because of their limited time.

"Sonya's dead? Why do they think I had anything to do with her death? I wouldn't hurt her like that, Tori." Trey was confused.

"Trey, you were found unconscious next to her body with a gun in your hand." Victoria didn't get a chance to say anything else because Malinda returned with Dr. Sanders and Tanya.

"I need to examine Mr. Taylor so I need all of you to leave." Dr. Sanders needed to get Trey's vitals back under control. He rang for a nurse as the ladies left the room.

## Chapter Four

Almost all the family was at the hospital once Tanya told them Trey was awake. Trenton's sister Kara had arrived from Florida, but TJ was still missing in action. He hadn't visited his brother once since he's been in the hospital, but he did ask if he was going to be okay. The family was disappointed that TJ believed Trey was guilty and wanted to prosecute the case. The DA wasn't going to let that happen. He thought TJ wouldn't be able to do an effective job, plus there was a conflict of interest. TJ was privy to the evidence against Trey. That was one of the reasons why he thought Trey was guilty. Another reason was he was glad the golden child was going to be knocked off his pedestal.

Chief Marshall was in Trey's room questioning him along with one of the officers that arrived at the scene with the Chief. Victoria was also there making sure Trey's rights weren't violated since he was still incoherent. Tara couldn't wait to get into the room to visit Trey. She'd been working with Jerome to see what evidence they had against Trey. She was mad as hell at TJ and Talia because they had the nerve to think Trey might be guilty. She could understand TJ feeling that way since he was so jealous and petty, but Talia surprised her. Talia wasn't as close to Trey as Tara, but they did have a special relationship. Tara decided it was time to grill her dad to see why Chief Marshall was questioning Trey when he wasn't strong enough to be interrogated.

"Dad why is Chief Marshall bothering Trey when he's not strong enough to deal with an interrogation?"

"Baby girl, I don't like this situation neither, but Carl has to do his job." Trenton replied.

"Well that's stupid and unfair of them to question Trey in the state he's in. Linda said that he was confused." Tara continued.

"Victoria is the best attorney in the state. She isn't going to let Trey answer any questions that will be used against him."

"Tara stop giving your dad a hard time. He's just as upset as the rest of the family." Tanya hoped Trey would get better soon. Tara was going to be out of control if the charges aren't dropped.

"Well not everyone in the family has enough sense to know Trey didn't do anything to that crazy heifer." Tara rolled her eyes at Talia.

"Don't be rolling your damn eyes at me, little girl. I have a right to my own opinion. I didn't say Trey was guilty. I just want him to be able to tell us how he got himself into this situation." Talia couldn't stand her baby sister sometimes. She had a one-dimensional mind and anyone that looked wrong in Trey's direction she acted like a pit bull.

"Oh my God, Lia. I know you don't think Trey would do something like this. For heaven's sake he used to be a police officer." Malinda couldn't believe Talia would think Trey was guilty.

"All of you cut this mess out right now. Trey didn't commit this crime. Victoria will see that his name is cleared." Trenton was tired of his children arguing with each other; it was bad enough he had to deal with TJ who believed the evidence against Trey was so overwhelming he must be guilty. They all were happy to see Chief Marshall and Victoria come out of Trey's room. Victoria said Trey was tired but got permission to see everyone for ten minutes. Trenton told the family to go in to see Trey while he stayed behind to talk to the Chief and Victoria. Chief Marshall had sent his officer back to the station after Trey made his statement.

"What are we looking at, Victoria?" Trenton didn't like to mince words when something this important was at stake.

"As we expected, Trey was charged with first degree murder. Dr. Sanders said he was doing better, so unfortunately he'll be cuffed to his bed and the guard will continue to be posted at his door."

"Carl, you know good and damn well Trey didn't commit this crime. I know he gave you a hard time when he was on the force, but he's a good kid." Trenton was doing his best to create doubt with the police.

"Judge this case has nothing to do with Trey's time on the force. He's being charged because of the evidence not my personal feelings." Carl explained.

"Victoria, I think Carl should be removed from this case because of his personal relationship with Sonya and her parents and his animosity towards Trey. This is a conflict of interest. While you're at it we should also make sure Winston doesn't preside over the case. That lousy son of his has been a thorn in Trey's side for as long as I can remember."

"No disrespect, Judge Taylor, any law official assigned to this case would work it by the facts not personal feelings." Carl had a problem with what Trenton was trying to do.

"In a real world that may be the case. You may be able to put your personal relationship aside, but I WILL NOT let my son be railroaded into a crime he didn't commit because of any personal problems someone may have against him." Trenton said forcefully.

"Let's table this for now. Trenton if you have time after your visit with Trey, I need to have a sit down with you." Victoria wanted to get the Chief out of there before Trenton pushed too hard and made things worse for Trey.

"I'll be back in a couple of days to see if Trey is more coherent." Carl shook Trenton and Victoria's hand before taking his leave.

"Trenton, I can meet with you later this evening with Trey. He wants you to be privy to every detail of the case. I know other family members may want to be involved, but the less the better. Plus, I was trying to get you away from Chief Marshall because you were walking a thin line."

"What's wrong with me stating the facts? You know as well as I do there would be conflicts of interest if certain people like Carl and that idiot Winston were involved."

"We can't be pushy until I see what evidence they have on Trey. It's bad enough that ballistics came back that he was holding the murder weapon that killed Sonya."

"Victoria, I need to know right now before we go any further if you believe in my son's innocence."

"Yes, I do Trenton, but even if I didn't, I could still provide him a kick-ass defense."

"Well, I better get in there before my daughters' kill each other. This case hasn't even started, and the family is already at each other throats."

"I have to leave now, but what's up with Trenton Jr. trying to prosecute his brother's case?"

"As you get to know my family better you will realize that TJ has always been jealous of Trey, almost since Trey's birth."

Victoria shook her head. "Tell Trey I'll get back with him soon. Enjoy your visit." Victoria gave a last-minute wave to Trenton then left him to be with the rest of the family.

As soon as Trenton stepped into the room Tara asked. "Dad what's the next step in the case?"

"We're going to go now so Trey can rest. Victoria and I will be visiting later to plan a strategy." Trenton said ignoring Tara's question.

"I want to be there too." Tara said.

"Not this time baby girl. We have a lot of work to do. All of you need to say your goodbyes to Trey so he can spend a few minutes alone with Malinda." The family did as they were told, and they all went their separate ways to get on with their day. Jerome told Trey he, Tara, and Trevor would be working together before he left the room.

## Chapter Five

The Taylor family sat in the courtroom on Friday morning awaiting the start of Trey's arraignment hearing. It hurt them badly to see Trey brought into the courtroom with his hands and feet shackled. He was released from the hospital that morning and taken directly into custody. He looked much stronger now that he was out of the hospital. The family had an emotional day with him yesterday knowing today would bring so much pain and misery. Trey's side of the courtroom was filled with his many supporters that included family and friends. Beverly (Trey's executive assistant) gave Trey a thumbs up sign when he was brought into the courtroom. On the other side right behind the prosecution's table sat Sonya's parents. All morning long, Christopher Young was giving the family an evil eye while Sharon Young just seemed to be uncomfortable.

Trey would have his prelim hearing right after the arraignment hearing. Victoria had to work her magic because Trenton was determined his son wasn't going to spend one day in jail. He wouldn't be safe there after all the criminals he'd arrested along with other criminals he ran across in his line of work. Of course, the prosecution would fight tooth and nail to see that bail was denied. Chris was livid when Trey was granted bail with all the evidence the state had against him. His not guilty plea was laughable to Chris. They knew Trenton was going to use his power to try and run this case. Carl had told them how Trenton had tried to get him thrown off the case. The same with Judge Winston, he made sure that he wasn't going to be the presiding judge.

Trey was taken back into custody until his bail was paid. His family and friends were so relieved he would be able to go home. Tanya and Talia tried to get Malinda to stay home but were unsuccessful. She looked tired around the eyes. She had been staying with her dad while Trey was in the hospital but looked forward to going home since Trey was being released. The family planned to meet up at Trey and Malinda's house, so after Trey was escorted out of the courtroom the family left to help Malinda get everything ready. Trenton and Trevor stayed behind with Victoria to take care of the bail. Tara was upset again when her dad wouldn't let her stay. She complained he was playing favorites by letting Trevor stay. Jerome also stayed with Trenton and Trevor. There was still no sign of TJ. Trenton figured he was somewhere pouting about not being able to prosecute his brother's case.

About two hours after they hauled Trey out of the courtroom he walked into the lobby where everyone was waiting for him. Trenton was the first to give Trey a big hug followed by a half hug from Trevor and Jerome. Trey looked like he aged in the few hours it took them to make bail. Victoria told him to go home and enjoy his family because tomorrow was a new and big day for them to start preparing his case. Trey and Trenton tried to get her to go with them, but she said she wanted to start preparing for the case and to bring her co-counsel up to speed. After the men were settled into Trenton's black on black Ford Flex, Trenton asked Trey to be honest and let them know how he was feeling.

"Dad, I don't know how this happened. The more I try to remember the more my head hurts." Trey was still in shock at what happened to him over the last few days.

"Son, you need to relax. Try not to force your memories. Someone did a real number on you." The doctors told the family that it may take a while for Trey to get his memory back so Trenton didn't want him to stress out about something he couldn't change.

"Guys, I don't know exactly what happened, but I do know I didn't kill Sonya. She got on my last nerve with her psycho behavior, but I wouldn't hurt her physically." Trey hoped his family and best friend believed him.

"Man, we know you didn't do this, but we have a tough fight on our hands because someone has gone to lot of trouble to frame you." Jerome knew his best friend since they were born and were raised like brothers. He had complete faith in Trey's innocence.

"Thanks, JW. I'm so glad to have you guys in my corner. Where's TJ? I didn't see him in the courtroom earlier." Trey had a puzzled look on his face.

"Don't worry about that fool. He'll probably be at the house when we get there." Trevor knew they would have to let Trey know that TJ didn't believe he was innocent and that he tried to prosecute his case.

It would hurt even more to find out Talia wasn't a hundred percent sure he was innocent.

"Now I get it. TJ doesn't believe I'm innocent." It didn't take Trey long to figure that out.

"Well not exactly. As matter of fact you need to know he fought hard to prosecute the case." Trenton didn't want to tell his youngest son that his oldest son wasn't on his side, but he knew Trey would find out sooner rather than later.

"Wow, if my own brother believes I'm guilty how are we going to convince a jury I didn't do it?" Trey said.

"Don't worry about that, Trey. Victoria is the best. She will clear your name."

"I think I'm going to rest my head for the rest of the drive." Trey closed his eyes to try to forget about all his troubles and prayed his wife wouldn't get too stressed out.

The next morning Trenton and Trey sat in Victoria's office. She went over the family history she'd gotten from Trenton and asked if he had anything else to add before they moved on to the next step. She told Trey since he was having trouble with his memory, he was going to have to see a therapist to help him to regain it as soon as possible. Trey didn't like this idea at all but knew he didn't have a choice. That was the last place he wanted to be. He hated leaving Malinda today; she looked so tired and stressed out. When she went to bed early last night with a house full of company, Trey knew she was in bad shape. He felt her tossing and turning all night and when he tried to hold her, she gently pushed him away. Trey was worried she had doubts about his innocence.

"Trey, I want to be perfectly honest with you. If I didn't know you personally, I wouldn't have taken this case. The state has overwhelming evidence that would make any sane person find you guilty." This is the first time in Victoria's career that she felt she may not be able to win a case. She only lost one case in her first year as an attorney, so she pushed herself to the limits to make sure there wouldn't be a second loss.

"I don't know what to say, Tori." Trey said.

"Wait a damn minute it sounds like you're giving up before you even get started." Trenton didn't like Victoria's defeatist attitude.

"Of course, I'm not giving up, Trenton. I just wanted to be up front with both of you about the evidence that's stacked against Trey. I need you to be honest with me Trey. Were you having an affair with Sonya?"

"No, Tori. I wouldn't do that to my wife. I love her more than anything."

"What's the last thing you remember about that day, Trey? It's time for us to create a timeline. Hopefully you'll get your memory back sooner rather than later."

"I remember arriving at the office and was surprised I was the first one there. Bev is usually there before JW or I get in."

"What time did you arrive at the office that morning?"

"It had to be right before seven o'clock because I remember turning the car off after I listened to Nephew Tommy's prank phone call on the radio."

"Do you remember anything after that?" Victoria asked. This didn't look good for no one to be at the office to provide Trey with an alibi.

"No everything else is a blank." Trey searched his memory but couldn't give Victoria any additional details.

"This isn't good, Trey. According to Beverly and Jerome statements you weren't at the office when they came in and it didn't look like you had been there that morning."

"I don't know what to say. I vaguely remember coming into the office. I don't know why everything else is a blank. We can review the security cameras."

"Ok, let's move on. When was the last time you remember seeing Sonya?"

"I don't know."

"What do you mean you don't know, Trey?"

"Just what I said, Tori. I can't remember the last time I saw Sonya."

"I think that's enough for now. I'll be going to your evidentiary hearing first thing Monday morning. You don't have to be there. I'll let you know how things turn out once I get back into the office. I need you to go home to rest, Trey. Take this weekend to do some relaxation exercises. Maybe you can get with Trevor to see if he can help you with exercises to help you to relax."

"Thanks, Victoria. I'll drop Trey off at home and check into setting him up with an appointment to see a therapist." Trenton had a feeling what was going on in Victoria's mind. Trey wasn't going to be able to help with the defense if he doesn't remember pertinent details. Leaving Victoria's office Trenton went into the house with Trey to find Malinda and Talia sitting at the kitchen table. Trey spoke to the ladies gave Malinda a brief kiss on her lips then went upstairs to take a nap. Trenton made a quick exit, so he wouldn't have to explain to the ladies that Trey's case wasn't looking good.

## Chapter Six

Monday afternoon Trenton and Trey sat in Victoria's office waiting for her to return. They didn't like the look on her face when she walked into her office. This was the day Trey will find out the evidence the state has against him. The weekend didn't fare any better than the previous days since the murder. Trey still didn't know what happened since the day he walked into his office and waking up in the hospital with a murder charge hanging over his head. He tried his best to stay cheerful and positive for Malinda's sake, but it was hard since he had the feeling that she was holding back on him. He wondered if she thought he was guilty. Before he could get any further in his thoughts, Victoria took the seat behind her big cherry oak desk.

"Trey it looks like you haven't rested much since the last time we met." Victoria could see the fatigue in Trey's eyes.

"It's hard to rest, Tori when I'm facing a murder charge with no memory of why I was at the scene."

"Trey, I asked you at our last meeting if you were having an affair with Sonya and you told me no. Would you like to rethink that question?"

"No, I don't, Tori, damn it. Why do you keep asking me that question? I haven't had a physical relationship with Sonya since we broke up years ago."

"Well, there's evidence at that condo where the two of you were found that leads one to think you guys were romantically involved."

"What kind of evidence?" Trenton didn't like where this was going.

"In one of the bedrooms there were candles and a small feast of half eaten food. According to Sonya's autopsy, the contents of the foods were still in her stomach."

"Listen, Tori. I'm going to tell you this one more time. I wasn't having an affair with that crazy woman and I most definitely didn't take part in a romantic feast with her." Trey was getting frustrated.

"Trey there was powder burns on your hand that came from the gun that killed Sonya. We're waiting on the results from the semen test."

"Oh my God, what the hell is going on here? I feel like the walls are closing in on me." Trey stood from the chair and began to pace around Tori's office.

"Son, you have to calm down." Trenton couldn't stand to see the helpless look on Trey's face.

"That's not all, Trey. The condo was leased in your name." Victoria was crestfallen when she saw all the evidence against Trey.

"I didn't lease a damn condo. We need to get JW and Tara in on this right now to see what the hell is going on here. This case is putting too much stress on Linda."

"I think that's a good idea, Trey. I have one of my best attorneys as co-counsel, but the prosecutor feels his case is so strong that he won't even consider a plea."

"Who said anything about a plea? My son isn't copping a plea. You need to prove his innocence." Trenton said.

"Trenton, I believe in Trey's innocence, but we have to face the fact that the state has a powerful case against him. Trey, I know you don't want to hear this, but you need to tell Malinda about the evidence."

"Are you crazy, Tori? I can't tell her in her condition that the state is trying to make it seem like I was having an affair with the woman that has been terrorizing us for years."

"Come on, Trey. You know how this works. When this hits the press they're going to have a field day. Reporters are going to be following your every move. It's not helping that Sonya's dad is running his own 'Lock Trey Up' campaign."

"That man is a damn fool. He should have gotten help for his daughter instead of blaming Trey for her psycho behavior." Trenton said.

"That's neither here nor there, Trenton. We must devise a plan to comeback the negative press Trey is receiving. Malinda is going to play a big role in this because they are going to hound her as much as Trey." That was all Victoria was able to say on the matter when Trey's cell phone began to ring. He looked down and saw that it was Talia and sent it to his voicemail. When a few minutes later Trenton's phone rang with Talia on the other end he answered, and all Trey and Victoria could understand was Talia was upset. When Trenton ended his call, he turned to Trey then said they had to get to his house right away. Leaving Victoria's office in a rush and arriving home in twelve minutes instead of the normal twenty the men were shocked to see reporters standing outside the gate that rushed over to them as soon as Trey and Trenton exited the car.

"Mr. Taylor, how long have you been having an affair with Ms. Young?" Other reporters were pushing microphones and cameras in Trey's face asking similar questions. Pushing pass, the reporters and hurrying into the house, Trey came face to face with an angry Talia.

"How could you, Trey. Your affair with Sonya is all over the place. Your wife is upstairs in tears refusing to come out of the bedroom."

"I didn't have an affair with Sonya or anyone else. I love my wife. Now get the hell out of my face, Lia." Trey ran past Talia to the bedroom he shared with Malinda.

"You should be ashamed of yourself, Talia. You know your brother wouldn't do anything to her hurt his wife." Trenton was upset that Talia was taking the same attitude as TJ.

"Well, tell that to the lady upstairs crying her eyes out." Talia wanted to say more, but Tara and Jerome walked through the door. Tara rolled her eyes at her sister then headed further into the entryway.

"What is Ms. Negativity complaining about this time, Dad?" Tara couldn't stand her older sister sometimes.

"Don't start, Tara. Your sister is upset because she's worried about Malinda and the baby." Trenton tried to keep peace between his two daughters.

"So is the rest of the family. That doesn't mean she should turn on our brother like TJ's sorry behind."

"This isn't going to help. I'm so glad both of you are here. We have a lot of ground to cover in a short amount of time. The state has strong evidence against Trey. Until he gets his memory back, we're going to have to take the lead. I have Trey set up for therapy tomorrow morning to see if that would help him regain his memory." Trenton figured he would have to get Trey a therapist, so he worked on that over the weekend.

"Dad what do they have against, Trey?" Tara asked.

"Let's go have a seat and I'll fill you both in on our meeting with Victoria." Trenton, Tara, and Jerome went into Trey's family room to have their conversation. They left Talia in the entryway.

Malinda finally let Trey into their bedroom, but he'd been trying to get her to talk to him for the last fifteen minutes. He knew she was hurt and that she was having doubts about his relationship with Sonya by the way she acted since he's been home. The entire weekend she did her best to avoid him and was brief in her answers when he tried to get her to talk to him. He missed having physical contact with her. They hadn't touched each other but a few times since his release. Now sitting next to her on the loveseat in her sitting room in their master suite, Trey was running out of ways to communicate with his wife.

"Trey, I need you to look me in my eyes and tell me the truth. Were you having an affair with Sonya?" Silent tears were running down Malinda's face as she asked this question.

"Baby, I swear to you on our child's life. I haven't had a physical relationship with Sonya since we broke up years ago."

"Somethings not adding up, Trey. Why was she so obsessed with you?"

"I don't know. I didn't give her any reason to act the way she was acting. I tried by best to distance myself from her. You know this, baby."

"Lia isn't a hundred percent sure of your innocence."

"Well if she feels that way, I need her to stay away from both of us. The state has a strong case against me. I don't need my own family doubting my innocence. She can go take a seat next to TJ." Trey was still upset that his oldest brother hadn't reached out to him and believes he's a cold-blooded murderer.

"Trey, you can't get mad at Lia. She had a front row seat of your toxic relationship with Sonya. She thought you would never get over your feelings for that woman."

"Baby, I'm doing all I can to remember what happened. Dad has me scheduled for therapy tomorrow morning. What I need to know is no matter what you hear that you believe me when I tell you I didn't have an affair with Sonya. I most certainly didn't kill her."

"I believe you, Trey. It's just hard with everything in the media saying the opposite." Trey and Malinda jumped a little when they heard a commotion downstairs. Getting up and giving each other a big hug, they headed downstairs in a united front to see what was going on.

## Chapter Seven

Trey sat with Trevor the next morning at his appointment with the therapist. He wondered why his dad hired women for his attorney and therapist. His dad explained to him that it would be better for him to have mostly women working his case. His dad knew both women had stellar reputations for getting the job done. Trey's mind traveled back to last night when he and Malinda had to fight with her dad to convince him that she should stay at home instead of moving back in with him until Trey's trial was over. Malinda convinced Trey to go upstairs since he had a headache and was frustrated over not getting his memory back. The dizziness and nausea were also getting the best of Trey. About an hour after sending Trey upstairs and after sending everyone home, Malinda joined Trey in their master bedroom.

*"Your dad doesn't believe I'm innocent, baby." Trey said.*

*"It's not that, Trey. He's just worried about me and the baby."*

*"I understand, but for him to suggest you move back into his house hurts. I'm also worried about his relationship with my parents. He's been friends with them for many years. I don't want this to tear them apart."*

*"They have to work that out for themselves, Trey. We have to find out who leased that condo in your name that set all of this into motion."*

*"Tara and JW have been working on the tapes from that day. I'll be meeting with them after I get my head shrunk in the morning."*

*"Trey, I know it's hard. Try to relax. Take your medication that should help you with your headaches and memory."*

From a distance Trey heard his name being called. He put last night behind him. Trey and Trevor was escorted into Dr. Westbrook's office. The office was nice and big with a welcoming feel to it. Trey didn't know what it was, but as soon as he stepped into the office, he felt a sense of peace. Dr. Westbrook was sitting behind her desk with two plush chairs in front of it. She waved her hand for Trey and Trevor to take a seat in the empty chairs.

"It's nice to meet you, Mr. Taylor. Just relax while I get your chart started." Dr. Westbrook normally used this tactic to observe the patient. She knew more than enough about why Trey was there and the protocol that would be the most effective treatment.

"I would like to begin by saying we should have results shortly regarding your memory loss. The drugs are out of your system so mainly we need to address the concussion. How have you been feeling?" Dr. Westbrook asked.

"My head still hurts. The few times I took the medication I couldn't function, so I don't want to take them any longer. I brought my brother with me today because he's been working with me on physical remedies that's more appropriate and should work better."

"That's a good start. Have you thought about your condition as being voluntary because you don't want to face what happened on the day in question?"

"If you're asking if I've intentionally blocked out what happened Dr. Westbrook, because I was having an affair with Sonya then the answer is NO." Trey was getting upset because he was so sick of people accusing him of cheating on Malinda.

"Trey calm down. Dr. Westbrook is here to help you not to place blame." Trevor knew Trey was frustrated. Trey has been short tempered and agitated since the case started.

"It's alright, Mr. Taylor. It's normal for a patient in Trey's position to feel helpless. May I call you, Trey?"

"Yes, and you can call my brother, Trevor since he may be coming to future appointments with me."

"Speaking on that subject, Trey, if you prefer to have a private session, let me know so that could be arranged."

"What I'm hoping is that we can move right into hypnosis or whatever you plan on doing with me, so I can find out what happened to Sonya."

"Let me start by letting you know you have amnestic syndrome amnesia. This form of amnesia impairs a person's ability to remember facts, events, experiences, and personal information. You shouldn't be alarmed if you have difficulty remembering new information because that won't last long. Your general knowledge, focus, intelligence, judgment, language skills, and personality will not be impaired." Dr. Westbrook was looking at the confused look on Trey's face.

"How long are we talking, days, weeks, months?" Trey wanted instant answers.

"I can't answer that for sure, Trey. What we can start off with is lifestyle changes. Make sure the people you're around are aware of your problem, so they will be patient; avoid hurrying (rushing can lead to frustration); try to follow your normal routine; and use memory aids such as PDAs (personal digital assistants), calendars, lists, etc."

"Well that should be easy since I'm only around my family and close friends."

"We can also use memory training techniques that can teach you how to organize, process, and build on the information taken in. These methods along with the physical program you're working on with your brother should bring positive results in no time." Dr. Westbrook explained.

"Ok, I see that our time is almost up. Thank you for your help, Dr. Westbrook." Trey wanted to get out of there, so he could meet with Tara and Jerome.

"No problem, Trey. Just stop by the front desk to set up your next appointment." Trey and Trevor left Dr. Westbrook's office and headed to Trey's office after setting up his next appointment for Friday morning.

While Trey and Trevor was at the therapist office Trenton and Tanya was having a private meeting with TJ and Talia. They were upset with them because of their lack of support for Trey. Even though they kind of understood where TJ was coming from Talia was a total surprise to them. They understood she was close to Malinda and wanted to protect her, but Trey was her blood and that should count for more. TJ got the conversation started once they were all seated in the family room.

"Mom, Dad, I know why you guys are meeting with us. It's unfair for you to expect us to blindly believe in Trey's innocence with all the evidence that points at his being guilty."

"Come off of it, TJ. You know damn well that evidence can be misleading. Why would Trey want to physically harm Sonya let alone kill her?" Trenton wasn't going to let TJ hide behind evidence when he knew what TJ was feeling was totally personal.

"Guys, it's not that I don't believe Trey is innocent. It's just he had a hard time shaking loose from Sonya. It was plain to see he still had feelings for her, and Linda is suffering because of his feelings for Sonya." Talia was sure that Trey wasn't a murderer, but regarding the affair it was hard to get around all the evidence against him.

"Talia, that's beside the point. Trey needs his family to stick by him. All the bad press he's getting he'll be lucky to keep the clients he already has let alone attract new business." Tanya looked at Talia as she spoke these words. She had a feeling Talia knew something they didn't about Trey's relationship with Sonya.

"I don't give a damn what the press, evidence, or anybody else says. Trey didn't do this and we're going to prove his innocence. We're going to have a dinner party here on Friday night where there will be important people here that will help Trey's case. TJ, I don't want to hear about you lobbying to try this case. We expect you to be here for the party. Talia you're to stop all this nonsense fighting with your sister and give Trey the support he needs. Do I make myself clear?" Trenton hadn't been this upset in a long time so hearing that he was sick of their lack of support for Trey put fear in both TJ and Talia.

"Yes sir. Both TJ and Talia answered at the same time. TJ hadn't seen Trey since he's been charged. He knew it was time for him to reach out to his baby brother even though he still had doubts about his innocence. He believed Trey was seeing Sonya behind Malinda's back even though he wasn't sure that he was responsible for her death.

"Talia, I want you and Tara to meet with me tonight, so we can go over some last-minute plans for the dinner party. I hope we don't have to have this conversation again." Trenton and Tanya left their children to ponder what they had just talked about then went upstairs to their bedroom.

"I guess we better get with the program, Lia." TJ said before he left the room.

## Chapter Eight

Trey was getting ready to leave for the office early the next morning. This week was going by slow, but now that it was Wednesday he hoped they would get more done on his case. Talia came by earlier to pick Malinda up for her doctor's appointment and to Trey's surprise she came into his home office and gave him a big hug.

*"Trey, I apologize for making it seemed like I don't believe in your innocence."*

*"Thanks, Lia. It's good to know you have faith in me." Trey responded. Malinda and Talia left a few minutes later.*

As Trey was walking towards the front door the doorbell rang. He was surprised because they usually didn't have unexpected visitors. Opening the door and seeing his oldest brother, TJ on the other side gave Trey mixed feelings.

"Hi, baby brother. I guess you're surprised to see me this morning?"

"Yes, I am. It's been a while, TJ." Trey didn't know what else to say.

"Trey, I want to apologize for being MIA. Do you have a few minutes to chat?" TJ half expected Trey to say no, but then thought about how that would be his reaction if Trey treated him like a criminal not Trey's.

"Sure, come in. Can I get you something to eat or drink?" Trey offered.

"No, I'm good, man. I know you heard I tried to prosecute your case. The only thing I can say is I'm sorry. I've spent most of my life trying to get dad to love me unconditionally like his relationship with you." TJ only wished Trey was guilty, but in his heart, he knew his baby brother wouldn't do anything like what he was being accused.

"TJ, what are your thoughts about my case?" Trey wanted to determine where TJ's head was at. He decided not to comment on TJ's first statement about their dad.

"I'll be honest with you, Trey. In my gut I feel you're innocent, but when I look at the evidence my head tells me there's no way for you to be innocent under the circumstances."

"That's fair enough. I appreciate you coming by, but Tara and JW are waiting for me at the office."

"Ok, Trey. Thanks for talking to me. Let me know if there's anything I can do to assist with your case."

"Will do. Have a good day, TJ." Trey and TJ walked out the door together going in separate directions leaving a puzzling feeling in Trey's gut.

Later that afternoon Trey sat in the conference room at his office with Tara and Jerome. They were just as frustrated as Trey about the lack of evidence they were able to gather to clear Trey's name. Trey and Trenton had an appointment in the morning with Victoria to go over his case. He still couldn't remember anything. He was going to ask Victoria if he should get hypnotized to see if that would jog his memory. Working out with Trevor seems to be controlling his headaches. Trevor had Trey doing Yoga and meditation exercises every day to ease his pain. He was blessed to have Trevor in his life to help him mentally and physically. He didn't want to depend on drugs to get him through the day. Tara and Jerome were just as important to Trey. They were working day and night to clear his name. Trey decided to take a break and tell Tara and Jerome about Talia and TJ's visits earlier that morning.

"Something strange happened this morning. As a matter of fact, two things. The first was when Talia dropped by to take Linda to her doctor's appointment, she gave me a big hug and apologized for not supporting me from the beginning." Before Trey could tell them about TJ's visit Tara interrupted him.

"Well it's about doggone time she came to her senses. I don't know what's her problem been lately, but she is getting on my last nerve. Don't think she came to her senses on her own. Mom and Dad came down hard on her and TJ for acting stupid yesterday." Tara knew her parents would get tired of the way Talia and TJ were acting and put their foot down.

"Oh, so that's why my second strange event this morning had to do with TJ stopping by my house." Trey was getting a clearer picture now about Talia and TJ's change of hearts.

"Wow, man. Your parents must have really laid into them to get them to react so quickly." Jerome knew his godparents didn't play, but TJ usual pattern was to do what he wanted to do and to hell with everyone else.

"Well, I'm just glad Talia doesn't see me as the enemy any longer. As for TJ, I still get the feeling he believes I'm guilty and would prosecute the case if he was allowed." Trey was about to continue with his next statement when Beverly knocked on the door. "Come in, Bev."

"Sorry to bother you, Trey, but you have a visitor in the lobby."

"Who is it, Bev. I'm not expecting any visitors."

"She said her name was Dawn Nicholson."

"Send her in please."

Dawn was a young lady that looked to be in her late twenties. "Hi, Mr. Taylor. It's good to see you again. I was contacted by the police about the condo you guys rented from me on the upper west side." The stranger said.

"What are you talking about? I've never met you before." Trey was sick of having all sorts of shit thrown at him without any knowledge of what the hell was going on."

"Yes, we have, it was about two weeks ago, I'm Dawn Nicholson. You leased a condo and said that it was going to be a get-a-way." Dawn explained.

"Exactly when did my brother lease this condo, Ms. Nicholson?" Tara didn't like what she was hearing. She knew they had to hurry up and find out what was going on with Trey.

"Let me see. I have the documentation right here." Dawn sat her purse down on the conference room table and opened her black portfolio grabbing a handful of papers. While Dawn was looking for her paperwork, Trey looked at his schedule for the month of August that Tara and JW had complied for him.

"Ok, we talked on August fourteenth and you came into the leasing office that following Monday, August seventeenth." As Dawn rattled off those dates Trey was checking his schedule. He didn't have a phone log for the fourteenth, but on the seventeenth, he had a two hour outside appointment with no other details from nine to eleven o'clock. Seeing this Trey became nervous.

"Do you have the time we met on that day?" Trey prayed she didn't say that two-hour period because he was in the office the rest of the day until six o'clock.

"We met at nine-thirty in the morning for about an hour."

"What made you come by here today, Ms. Nicholson?" Trey was disappointed with that information.

"Well, I heard about your case in the media and felt bad for you and your wife. I had my daughter two years ago under stressful circumstances, so I wondered how your wife was handling the pressure."

"Wait a minute how did you know Trey's wife was pregnant?" Jerome was getting mixed feelings regarding Dawn's visit.

"Because he told me she's in her last trimester of a difficult pregnancy and figure a change of scenery would make her more comfortable." Dawn jumped a little when Tara got up from her seat and hugged her tightly while Trey and Jerome breathed a sigh of relief.

"Wait a minute. Why are you guys acting like you just won the lotto?" Dawn was confused by the trio's behavior. She handed the paperwork to Trey. He knew it was his signature on the paperwork, but still didn't understand why he went that route.

"May I have a copy of these documents?" Trey was still baffled.

"Sure, but I gave you a copy when you signed the lease." Trey had Beverly make a copy of the paperwork he received from Dawn and thanked her for coming in. When the trio was alone again Trey spoke up.

"I still don't know why I would lease a condo. None of this is making any sense."

"Man, we're just blessed that you gave her a reason for leasing whether it makes sense or not." Jerome and Tara had another lead they could follow. They also were in the process of doing a timeline.

"Big brother are you and Linda doing ok?" It didn't make sense to Tara why Trey would lease a condo. If he and Malinda wanted to get away, then they could have used the family's cabin.

"Yes, we're fine, but Linda has been kind of depressed since she had to take an early leave from work. The most logical thing would have been for us to go to the cabin if we needed to get away, not for me to lease a condo."

"That's something the prosecutor will bring up I'm sure." Jerome wondered where his friend's head was when he leased the condo.

"Thank you, guys, for all your help. I going to leave now so I'll be ready when Trevor gets here then head home. I want to be there when Lia bring Linda back home." Trey gathered some work papers and the lease, so he could show it to Malinda when she got home. Saying bye to his sister, best friend, and assistant, Trey left the office once Trevor arrived with a slight throbbing in his head.

## Chapter Nine

Trey and Trenton were sitting in Victoria's office the next morning as Trey told them about the meeting with Dawn. Trey still couldn't come to terms as to why he leased the condo and the look on his dad's face said the same. After his dad looked at the lease he handed it to Victoria. She asked Trey was he sure that was his signature on the contract. He confirmed that it was, so she started the discussion regarding the next step in the case.

"Trey, how have you been feeling?" Victoria wanted to start the conversation off light.

"Frustrated as hell. I don't have any idea why I would lease that condo. My memory is non-existence, my wife is stressed as more evidence against me is coming out, and if I didn't know better, I would say I was guilty." Trey responded angrily.

"We have to find out why you can't remember what happened that day, Trey. We do have on our side no eyewitnesses to the actual crime, but with the smoking gun in your hand and other circumstantial evidence we're fighting an uphill battle."

"Tell us something we don't know, Victoria." Trenton expected a better defense from Victoria.

"I have a status conference tomorrow and my co-counsel should have an update on Sonya's movements. We must work harder at tracking your movements too, Trey. The footage from your office on the morning of the murder didn't give us much to work with. I'll also file a continuous motion to give us more time to prepare, but Chris Young is pushing for a speedy trial"

"Tori, I was thinking about asking the therapist to hypnotize me to see if we can get quicker results. I know how Sonya's parents feel, but I attempted on many occasions to tell them how out of control Sonya had become. Mr. Chris was so busy blaming me he wouldn't hear anything I had to say."

"That's an option. I don't know if Dr. Westbrook will be willing to do this so early in your treatment. She may want to explore other options first. As for the parent's refusal to get Sonya the help she needed, that will help our case. We'll need a list documenting the dates you approached them." The look on Trenton and Trey's faces told Victoria that they didn't care; they just wanted fast results.

"Ok. I think I can narrow down the dates. Ms. Sharon was more understanding than her husband, but I know she's upset about their daughter's death."

"That fool is still trying to petition to get Winston as presiding judge. He is so full of bitterness that he's not thinking straight. I can see why his daughter had so many problems." Trenton felt sorry for Chris as a parent losing his only child, but that's as far as his sympathies would go. If they would have been more demanding in getting treatment for Sonya maybe she would still be alive and at the least she would've had a more stable existence.

"Trey, I know it'll be hard but go home to rest. Try to concentrate on your wife and baby." Victoria knew she needed to stall for time before the trial because physically Trey didn't look like he was ready. When Trey and Trenton left her office, Victoria called Reuben (her co-counsel) in so they could review the case.

Trenton took Trey over to his house after they left Victoria's office, so he could visit with his mom and have an early lunch. On the drive to the house they talked about the strange visit from Dawn. It didn't make sense why she would come in out the blue and pass along that information. Trey talked to Malinda last night about Dawn's visit. She didn't see the reasoning behind Dawn's visit and thought something else was going on. Trenton told Trey until he got his memory back, make sure he didn't go anywhere alone. Trey was getting sick of having someone to chaperone him everywhere he had to go. The only place he went alone was when he went to the office yesterday. When his dad found out he had a fit. As they pulled up into the driveway Trenton turned off the engine then turned towards Trey.

"Son, I know this is getting you down, but don't lose focus of the prize. You need to be prepared for the unexpected. Don't be surprised if Chris reaches out to you."

"I know, Dad, but as I was telling Tara and JW yesterday. If I didn't know better, I would say I was guilty with all the evidence stacked against me."

"You just said the magic word, stacked. Something isn't right with this case. I know we're dealing with more than one person that's framing you."

"The only people I could give Tori off hand that could be labeled as my enemies seem to have alibis. Malcolm was said to be out of town, Mr. Chris was at work, Linda's, Aunt Maria was off pouting in Florida, and Greg Timmons was incarcerated."

"Have Jerome to check them out again. We want to be sure of the people that have the most to gain if you were out of the picture thoroughly investigated."

"This Malcolm thing is so stupid. Even if Linda wasn't with me, she wouldn't go back to that immature fool."

"He should have gotten with Sonya since both of them are/were delusional."

"Dad, I want you to know I wasn't having an affair with Sonya. I admitted to Linda there were times even with the restraining order against her, Sonya still approached me, but I didn't report it. Of course, she was upset that I didn't, but she understood."

"If we can't get a continuation, we need to work harder on getting your memory back."

"I guess we better head in before mom comes out here with her belt." Trey laughed at the face his dad made then they went into the house to spend some quiet time together.

Later that evening Chief Marshall sat in front of Sonya's parents' house trying to get the courage to go in to talk to his best friends. Chris was upset with him because he wasn't at liberty to tell him about all the details of the case. Carl accepted a long time ago that his goddaughter had lost her way. Both Carl and his wife tried to help Sonya deal with her problems regarding Trey once he got married, but she wouldn't listen. The major news he was going to have to tell his friends were even if Sonya hadn't been murdered, she was going to die anyway because she had brain cancer. He wondered if that impaired her judgment to do the crazy things she was doing towards the end of her life. He knew Chris didn't know about the cancer or he would have told him. Going to the door and ringing the bell, Chris opened it so quickly Carl jumped back a little.

"Man, why the hell were you just sitting in the car like you didn't want to come in?" Chris looked like he aged ten years since Sonya's death.

"I was just trying to unwind from a rough day, where's Sharon? I need to talk to both of you guys together."

"She's in the kitchen fixing us a snack. Come have a seat in the living room." A few minutes after the men were seated, Sharon brought a tray out with cheese, crackers, fruit, and coffee. She asked Carl if he would like something different to drink, but he said coffee was fine. A few minutes later, Carl started the conversation with the reason for his visit.

"Guys, the autopsy report on Sonya came in today with the full results of her cause of death."

"About damn time since her funeral is tomorrow. We didn't need an autopsy to know the cause of death. Jackass Trey shot my baby to death." Chris wondered what took so long to get the result.

"The gunshot wounds were the primary cause of death, but the report also showed that Sonya was dying from brain cancer." The shocked looks on his best friends' faces broke Carl's heart.

"That can't be possible. She would have told us if she was sick." Sharon didn't want to believe her daughter would keep this information from them, but that would probably explain why she was acting so neurotic.

"Have you guys gone over to her apartment yet?" Carl figured his friends hadn't been over there yet because he was sure they would have found some information about Sonya's illness.

"No. We were planning on going over there on Sunday after church." Sharon was doing all the talking while Chris remained quiet.

"Sweetie, our baby may have been sick and didn't want us to know. About three weeks ago I received a strange call from a doctor's office and when I asked Sonya about it she said the call was a mistake and that she was helping out a sick friend." Chris said.

"Why didn't you mention this to me, Chris? This could explain why Sonya had so many problems and why she kept harassing Trey and Malinda." Sharon was disappointed Chris kept the phone call from her.

"Woman, I know damn well you're not blaming our baby for that bastard murdering her in cold blood." Chris was so mad he was shaking.

"Calm down, man. You're going to give yourself a heart attack." Carl wanted Chris to calm down, so they could finish their conversation.

"My wife needs to stop talking this foolishness. It wasn't our daughter's fault she was murdered." Chris continued.

"Come off it, Chris. We both knew there was something wrong with Sonya's mind. If Trey is responsible for her death then he needs to pay for it, but until we find out all the details, we need to know what happened to Sonya." Sharon was so tired of her husband acting like Sonya didn't have serious issues.

"This conversation is over. I'll talk to you tomorrow, Carl." Chris left the living room, went to the hall closet to grab a sweater then left the house.

"I'm sorry, Carl. That man wouldn't listen when Sonya was alive that she had problems, so I know it's going to take an act of God for him to listen now that she's not here to defend herself." Sharon said.

"I better get going. Be patient with him. I'll see you guys at the funeral tomorrow." Carl gave Sharon a brief hug then left to head home to figure out how he was going to let his friend know that things were more out of control with Sonya then they anticipated.

## Chapter Ten

Trey woke up Friday morning with no progress made on getting his memory back. His headaches were controllable since he's been working with Trevor. He only went to the office once since he found out about his leasing the condo. He wanted to stay close to home to keep an eye on Malinda. She wasn't a happy camper when he told her about the condo. He had a busy day ahead of him, first meeting with Dr. Westbrook then with Victoria and his dad later that morning. Malinda had just gotten out of the shower and entered the bedroom when Trey's cell phone rang.

"Good morning, baby sister."

"Good morning, Trey. I'll be taking you to your appointment this morning with Dr. Westbrook because Trev had to do something for mom and dad this morning." Tara said. Sometimes the siblings shorten each other names.

"You guys do know I can drive myself. I still don't see the need to have a chaperone everyplace I have to go." Trey was irritable about this situation.

"We're just trying to cover all the bases. We don't want anything to happen to you. While I have you on the phone can you talk dad into letting me join you guys when you meet with Victoria later this morning?"

"Why can't you ask him, baby sister?"

"Because you know he's going to say no if I ask him, but if you tell him that it would help me with some of the research Rome and I are doing, he'll be more likely to say yes." Tara sometimes shortens Jerome's name.

"Why do you want to attend the meeting, Tara?" Trey asked.

"Because I want to be privy to all the details not just what you and dad want me to know. I'll see you in about half hour." Tara ended their call. Trey went over to where his wife was sitting and gave her a big hug.

"Tara will be here in half an hour. Trev had to do something for mom and dad. She wants me to convince dad to let her meet with us later this morning when we meet with Victoria."

"I can't see him letting that happened unless you guys come up with a good reason."

"Do you need anything before I go take my shower?"

"No, I'm good, babe. Lia will be here shortly to help me with the nursery."

"Ok, take it easy." Trey left Malinda to ponder in her thoughts.

Trey was sitting in Dr. Westbrook's office with Tara. He was upset that Dr. Westbrook wouldn't do hypnosis on him. She tried to explain it was too early in his treatment to do hypnosis. Trey let her know how frustrating it was to have people chaperoning him every place he had to go and how disturbing it was he couldn't remember renting a condo. Dr. Westbrook sympathized with him but told him he was doing well because he had fewer headaches. She also told him his memory may come back to him all at once or in bits and pieces. She encouraged him to continue to work with Trevor because physical and mental exercises were important. Trey asked her a question he dreaded but had to know because sometimes he doubted himself.

"Dr. Westbrook is there a possibility I could have committed this crime then blocked it out?"

"Trey what are you saying? You know you wouldn't murder anyone." Tara didn't like it that Trey seemed to lose faith in his innocence.

"Tara, I just need to know. All the evidence points to my guilt, so I just need to know if that's why I don't have my memory back because I don't want to face what I've done."

"Trey, I can't give you an accurate answer to that question. The mind has a way of filtering information and protecting itself. What kind of relationship did you have with Sonya?"

"When we were together years ago, I loved her very much. She was my first love. We dated for almost two years." Trey explained.

"Ok, that was your early relationship with her, what about later when you were adults?" Dr. Westbrook needed to know about Trey and Sonya's recent relationship.

"Well, we broke up right before I went to Northwestern and when I finished my degree I hooked up with Linda (I met Linda before I started dating Sonya). Sonya came back into my life when I joined the police force at twenty. She knew I was with Linda, but she kept pursuing a relationship with me. She stalked me for about five years until I got fed up and got a restraining order against her. That didn't stop her from stalking me. I've had trouble in my marriage and with my family because I wouldn't report when she violated the order."

"Trey, I want to give you something to think about before our next visit on Tuesday. Try to think about the last time you saw Sonya and what was the nature of contact. It may help if you find a quiet place and take a few hours to explore your memory. If you don't have anything else, you want to share I'll see you on Tuesday."

"I have just one more question. I know I wasn't supposed to, but I tried to contact Sonya's parents. Her funeral is tomorrow, and I wanted to pay my respects, but they don't want me anywhere near them or their daughter."

"I know you understand what they're feeling right now, Trey. You may think it would jog your memory, but in this case the best advice I can give you is to stay far away from her family, so they can have time to heal."

"Thank you, Dr. Westbrook. I'll see you next week. Enjoy your weekend." Trey and Tara left then headed towards Victoria's office. Trey was surprised Tara didn't give him a harder time when he told her their dad said she couldn't meet with Victoria. Tara dropped him off and told him she would see him later.

Trenton was already at Victoria's office in the lobby when Tara dropped Trey off. "How much trouble did your sister give you when you told her she couldn't come to the meeting, Trey?"

"It was strange, Dad. She didn't push at all." Trey responded. They stopped talking when Victoria's assistant showed them into her office about five minutes after Trey arrived. They both were glad to see she seemed to be in a good mood and prayed it had to do with the status conference she attended for his case. As soon as they were seated she got started.

"How have you guys been since we last met? How did your appointment go this morning, Trey?"

"We're good. You were right, Dr. Westbrook said it was too early in my treatment for her to use hypnosis."

"Sorry to hear that. Did anything happen in your session?" Victoria wanted to give Trey and Trenton time to relax.

"Well, Tara had to go with me because Trevor wasn't available. She kind of tripped out when I asked Dr. Westbrook if there was any way I could have committed this crime and blocked it out."

"Boy, what the hell is wrong with you. Of course, you couldn't have committed this crime. Don't think you would've gotten a different response if Trevor was there." Trenton was upset that Trey would have asked a question like that.

"Let's calm down, Trenton. Are you guys ready for an update?" Victoria continued when both Trenton and Trey nodded. "Your trial date has been scheduled for Monday, October Twelfth."

"You couldn't get a postponement?" Trenton was worried that wasn't enough time to prepare Trey's case.

"No, that's not an option right now, but I do have news about the autopsy. It seems Sonya had terminal brain cancer and only had a short time to live." Victoria said.

"Oh my God, that's horrible. Maybe that's why she was acting so psycho during her last days." Trey felt bad for the girl he fell in love with so many years ago.

"Don't you go feeling sorry for that lunatic. She's been crazy for years." Trenton said.

"Trey, I'm going to be real with you. You must let any compassionate feelings you have towards Sonya go. This is going to be a down and dirty trial and I need you to be prepared for the fight of your life." Victoria wanted Trey to get some of the harder feelings his dad had because they were going to have to drag Sonya's name through the mud to obtain Trey's freedom.

"Son, you got to toughen up. The prosecution is going to drag all of us through the mud to get a conviction."

"I know, Dad." Trey didn't want to blast Sonya because it would hurt her mom. Trey couldn't understand why his dad didn't have compassion for Sharon.

"Trey, we need to know that you didn't have any kind of personal relationship with Sonya." Victoria was starting to doubt Trey's non-involvement with Sonya.

"Why do you keep asking me about my relationship with Sonya, Tori? I told you I love my wife and wouldn't hurt her by cheating on her with anyone." Trey said angrily.

"Ok, now I think we have to look at this from a different angle. Suppose Sonya was working with someone and they set all of this into motion?" Victoria was thinking that Sonya plotting her last and darkest revenge by making sure Trey live the most miserable life possible.

"I know Sonya had her issues, but to devise a plan down to the very last detail like that she would have to be boarding on psychotic." Trey said praying Sonya hadn't gotten that bad off in her final days.

"Think about it, Trey. What would she have to lose? She didn't have much time, she refused treatment, and she kept her illness a secret." Victoria liked this line of thought more and more.

"I'll be damn. She got exactly what she wanted in the end: Coming between Trey and Malinda." Trenton could see the point in Victoria's theory.

"Ok, I think it's time to end this for today. My head is beginning to hurt." Trey said while rubbing his temples.

"Sure, take it easy, Trey." Victoria said as she watched Trey and Trenton leave her office. This was the first time since taking Trey's case Victoria found a light at the end of the rainbow.

## Chapter Eleven

Trey was glad that Talia came by to take Malinda shopping. He always dreaded Mondays, but today even more because the reality kind of sunk in that Sonya was really gone. His parents on behalf of the family sent flowers, but none of them attended the funeral over the weekend. Trey had mixed feelings about the funeral. He wanted to go on the one hand, but on the other he knew it would hurt Malinda and make things more difficult for Sonya's parents. He was planning on going into the office later that morning to work on a few of his open cases. Tara and Jerome along with Beverly had been holding down the office while he was out of commission. Thinking about when he first started dating Sonya, he went back to his junior year in high school.

Trey was on top of the world after being nominated for home coming king. He was even more excited that Sonya the most popular girl in school and his girlfriend was nominated for queen. They had been dating for a few months and were hopelessly in love. Sonya wasn't the first girl Trey dated, but she was the first girl he loved. They made a great couple with both having an outgoing personality, popularity in and outside of school, and had the same goals of wanting to work in law enforcement. Trey wanted to be a police officer while Sonya's dream was to be an FBI agent.

To both of their surprises their relationship started to fizzle when they graduated from high school. Trey went off to Northwestern that fall while Sonya wanting to take a year off from school didn't register for fall classes. They mutually ended their relationship to pursue other goals. Trey focused on his studies. That was a busy year for Trey because he not only joined the police academy, he also started dating Malinda Paige Roberts. He first met Malinda during his sophomore year in high school but didn't have any romantic interest in her at the time.

He had been dating Malinda for over a year when Sonya came back into his life. He had lost track with her over the years. She had changed so much and didn't have the spark about herself like she had during their high school years. He found out she didn't go to school and ended up hanging around the wrong crowd. She pursued Trey even though she knew he was in a committed relationship. It had gotten so bad he had to get a restraining order to keep her away from him and Malinda after they were married. He remembered she went off her rocker when she found out he and Malinda were engaged. The ringing of Trey's cell phone brought him back to the present. The call was from a restricted number, so he started not to answer.

"Hello this is Trey."

"When are you going to do the right thing and let Lynn go?" The angry voice on the phone was one Trey didn't want to hear from.

"What do you want, Malcolm?" Trey asked impatiently.

"I want you to do right by Lynn. Set her free so she can make a life with someone who will treasure her and her baby the way they deserve."

"I supposed that someone is you right?" Trey asked.

"You damn right it is. I've loved that woman for years and if you hadn't interfered in our relationship, we would still be together."

"You're delusional, man. You guys had already broken up before I started seeing her. This is old news. We're married now with a baby on the way. You need to get on with your life and leave us alone."

"Never, you're going to prison for the rest of your sorry ass life for offing the woman you should have been with all along." Malcolm said.

"This conversation is over. Don't contact me or my wife again." Trey disconnected the call. He decided it was time for him to go into the office, so he could do something productive. He could hear the housekeeper downstairs. A few minutes later he texts Tara to let her know he was ready for her to pick him up. Going downstairs Trey waited for Tara and decided to put the past and Malcolm's call out of his head.

Trey was quiet on the ride into the office. Tara had a worried look on her face because she didn't know why her brother was behaving that way. She knew he was down about not being able to say goodbye to Sonya, but as their dad explained to him that was for the best. Tara was beginning to worry about Trey not having even a glimpse of his memory come back to him. She hoped Dr. Westbrook would agree to Trey's hypnosis idea soon. As soon as Trey walked into the office and spoke to Beverly, he asked Tara and Jerome to meet him in the conference room.

"You guys won't believe who had the damn nerve to call me this morning. That sorry ass Malcolm." Trey was still mad that fool had the nerve to call him. To think that he would step aside and let that fool have his wife and child was absurd.

"Wow, it's been a while since you mentioned his name." Jerome knew at one time Malcolm was giving Trey and Malinda as many problems as Sonya.

"What did he say to you, Trey to make you so upset?" The look on Trey's face made Tara think he was ready to punch something or somebody.

"He told me if I cared about Linda, I should set her free so she can start a new life for her and her baby with someone who really treasures her."

"Ok, needless to say that someone to step in would be him." Tara said.

"Right on the first guess. He also took the pleasure of saying since I'm going to be gone for the rest of my sorry ass life it's only fair."

"Well, guess who just jumped to the head of my suspects list." Tara thought about Malcolm when this first happened, but since he was an attorney and his dad a judge, she figured he wouldn't be so stupid.

"Speaking of suspects and someone I hadn't heard about in a long time, Greg Timmons. He still holds me responsible for his first bit in prison. The last I heard he was drinking himself to death."

"Now he's a spooky creature." Tara remembered the trouble he caused Trey once he was released from prison.

"This is getting to be a bit much. None of the prime suspects are panning out, but I'm not ready to cross any of them off the list just yet." Trey knew that any of them could have conspired with Sonya to do her dirty work.

"I want to keep the person that called the report in on our list too." Jerome was getting a funny feeling in his stomach about the caller. Trey may have been the person with the best instincts in the firm, but this time Jerome smelled something fishy.

"Tori said they did a thorough check on her and she came up clean." The woman that called to report hearing shots fired lived in the condo to the left of the one Trey leased.

"I'm going back to the timeline and it's not adding up. According to the coroner, Sonya's time of death was between seven and nine o'clock so why would the caller say she just heard the shots when she called in at ten forty-five?" That didn't make sense to Jerome.

"What time was it again that you guys tracked me leaving here that morning?" Trey was trying to put his detective skills to work even though he had a pounding headache.

"That would be seven forty-five. It's about a thirty-minute drive from here to the condo if you went straight there, so that's putting you arriving around eight-fifteen." Unfortunately, that puts Trey at the scene of the crime given the estimated time of death.

"Tori can tear that timeline apart. There is no way I could have driven up there, ate, had sex, and murdered her within forty-five minutes."

"Finally, you are getting it big brother." Tara had a big smile on her face.

"What are you talking about, baby sister? I know it may have confused you when I asked Dr. Westbrook about the possibility of me committing the crime and blocking it out, but I have to find some reasonable explanation as to why I'm not getting my memory back and leasing that damn condo."

"Okay, Trey it's time to get you back home. Lia and Linda should be there by now and by the look on your face you could use a little nap." Tara felt good about the ground they've covered. Now all she needed was for her dad to get her access to the crime scene, so she could do her own investigation.

"Sure sis. JW don't let this one lead you into something dangerous or illegal. She has a knack for getting in too deep." Trey and Tara left while Jerome planned on figuring out what their next move would be on the case. They worked like it was just another day when it was Labor Day. They should have been having festivities with their families.

## Chapter Twelve

Sitting in a dark room wondering how everything gotten out of control and trying to deal with the guilt was almost too much to handle. When the plan was first devised, it all seemed so simple and foolproof but as time went by simple was a thing of the past. Still thinking the decision made was the right decision somehow made it a little easier. Praying for absolution everyday will make it easier because God is more forgiving than humans.

The next phase of the plan was a little trickier to pull off but keeping sight of the goal will ensure justice will be served. Knowing that the target was suffering made the plan worthwhile. No one deserved to suffer more than, Trey Adrian Taylor. He was so used to getting what he wanted and walking over anyone that stood in his way. Those days were about to come to an end when he goes to prison for the rest of his life.

Now was the time to step up the plan and take control. Leaving anything up to faith wasn't an option. The case was moving too slowly. That fool has a strong support system that need to be torn apart. The evidence against him was astounding, but he still has people believing he was innocent. What more do they need than the smoking gun in his hand? Deciding to move to the next phase sooner than planned was risky but necessary. Trey would know what it's like to live in hell before this was over and done with.

It was now Wednesday more than two weeks since Sonya's murder and Trey was still no closer to getting his memory back. When he and Trevor went to his appointment yesterday with Dr. Westbrook, Trey's mood wasn't good. He told her he was tired of living in the dark and she needed to figure out a way for him to get his memory back. Although she sympathized with him, she continued to say it was too soon for hypnosis. Trey slept in that morning because he didn't feel like going into the office and he felt anxious, so he wanted to try some of the relaxation exercises Trevor taught him. Malinda wasn't at home, but he expected her soon because they had a doctor's appointment later that afternoon. They only had six weeks before their child will be born. They didn't want to know the sex even though their doctor seemed anxious for them to know. They will be happy with a healthy baby. Trey must have dosed off because the next thing he heard was banging on his front door. Going over to answer the door, Trey had no idea who would be so insistent.

"Ms. Sharon, what are you doing here?" Trey was surprised and kind of glad to get a visit from Sonya's mom.

"May I come in, Trey?" Sharon Young asked.

"Sure. I'm sorry for being so rude." Trey moved aside so Sharon could come through the door. He told her to have a seat in the living room.

"I need to hear from you that you didn't murder my baby, Trey."

"I sorry, Ms. Sharon. I can't talk about the case. All I wanted was for Sonya to get help and to have a good life. That's why I approached you and Mr. Chris on so many occasions."

"I know my child needed help. Did you know she was dying of brain cancer?"

"No, I didn't find that out until after all of this happened."

"Why wouldn't she tell us? I'm sure that's part of the reason why she was so out of control."

"I have no idea. I just wish she would have trusted someone, so she wouldn't have gone through that alone." Trey still felt sorrow for Sonya.

'Well, I won't take up any more of your time. Chris would have a fit if he knew I came over here to see you. Just for the record, Trey, I don't believe you murdered my daughter, but I do feel that you could have done more to break the hold you had on her heart."

"I promise you, Ms. Sharon, I wasn't leading Sonya on..." That was all Trey had a chance to say before Malinda and Talia walked into the living room.

"Hi babe. Ms. Sharon was just leaving." Trey was getting nervous with the evil look the ladies shot towards Sharon even though they did give her a pleasant hello before Trey walked her to the door. Trey didn't get a chance to get all the way into the living room before his wife started questioning him.

"What the hell was she doing here, Trey?" Malinda asked

"Calm down, babe. I think she just needed someone to talk to about Sonya's illness."

"Don't tell me to calm down, Trey. You shouldn't be talking to her under any circumstances. What if she was wired?" Malinda persisted.

"You're letting your imagination run wild. She didn't push me when I told her I couldn't talk about the case."

"Trey, Linda is right. That woman had no right coming over here talking to you. This smell fishy to me." Talia couldn't wait to tell their dad that woman dropped by out of the blue.

"Lia don't you start too. I feel sorry for her because her husband is consumed with so much hatred. I know she isn't getting any support from him."

"Well, I don't mean to sound mean, Trey but that's her problem not ours." Malinda was tired from her outing, so she went to sit on the sofa.

"Thanks for bringing her back home safely, Lia. She needs to rest before we go to her appointment later." Trey gave his sister a hug and walked her to the door. When he went back into the living room Malinda was sleep, so he went to the linen closet to get a thin blanket to cover her and headed upstairs to take a nap.

Kind of paranoid after his visit from Sharon, Trey went to pick up Malinda's baby sister Carmen to sit with her so he could go to the office to work with Tara and Jerome on the case. Trey knew Malinda would feel better now that her baby sister was back in town. Carmen had been away at summer camp for the last four weeks. Her brother CJ will be back in town on Saturday, so Malinda would have an even bigger support system. Trey had mixed feelings about CJ's return because he was upset that Trey's problems were causing his sister undue stress. Up until the murder, Trey had a good relationship with his in-laws. At twelve Carmen didn't get the full picture of the case and continued to have hero worship of Trey, but CJ and his dad knew the circumstances better, so they were kind of stand offish.

Trey was at the office twenty minutes after getting Malinda and Carmen settled. He loved his sister-in-law as much as his own sisters. She reminded Trey of Tara the way she unconditionally supported him. Tara and Jerome were in the conference room with their heads together while Beverly was at her desk typing away at a report, they wanted her to transcribe. Trey was cheerful as possible when he said hello.

"About time you showed your ugly mug around here." Jerome said with humor in his voice. He wanted to do something to put the smile back on his best friend's face.

"Look who's talking. A guy with a face that only a mother could love." Trey countered back at his best friend.

"Okay, if the two of you are done with hurling insults at each other we can get down to business." Tara tried to sound stern, but she was so worried they were not going to be able to prove Trey's innocence.

"Look who's trying to run things around here, JW." Trey liked to let his baby sister feel she's in charge sometimes.

"Better watch out man, she could send you out of here packing." The men like to mess with Tara because she was too serious sometimes.

"Are we going to get any work done today or not? I could always go harass my professor." Tara was ready to get down to business.

"How would you guys like to go on a field trip?" Trey felt it was time to visit the crime scene. Since he was the legal leaseholder of the condo, when the police released it, they told him he could have access. Plus, he was hoping some memories would return.

"Where are we going, big brother?" Tara asked.

"Someplace you've been itching to go for the last two and a half weeks?"

"What are we waiting on? Let's roll. I'm driving so you guys won't be rushing me to leave before I get all the information I need." Tara said happily.

"We better say our prayers that we make it there in one piece." Jerome said with humor in his voice.

Trey told Beverly where they were going and that they should be back in a couple of hours. Getting into Tara's Ford Fusion, candy apple red on the outside and black on the inside the guys relaxed while she drove to the condo. The car was a graduation gift from Tara's siblings when she graduated high school. She always fussed about not having a car while she was in high school, but her parents were dead set against her having one. They relaxed their minds while they headed to what they hoped to be another lead in the case.

## Chapter Thirteen

Trey and Malinda sat in Dr. Westbrook's office waiting for her to return. She barely had a chance to greet them when her assistant said she had to see her for a minute. While waiting for Dr. Westbrook to return, Malinda glanced sideways at Trey. She felt bad for her husband. Every time he thought something would jog his memory he was let down. Going to the condo the other day with Tara and Jerome didn't do anything for Trey but cause more frustration. They talked for a long time afterwards. Trey threatened to go to another therapist if Dr. Westbrook wouldn't agree to the hypnosis. At this point he felt that was his only option. With the trial fast approaching time was running out and he wanted to solve this mess before the trial started.

Malinda interrupted Trey's thoughts when she asked him, "Trey, are you going to have lunch with Trevor and TJ?"

"I don't know, Linda. Outside of that one time he came by the house, TJ hasn't even contracted me. I know Trevor's approach is to try to bring us together, but I'm not in the mood to hear any negative shit come out of TJ's mouth."

"Trey it may be good for you to talk to TJ."

"How can you say that Linda when I know he thinks I'm guilty as sin?" Trey asked.

Dr. Westbrook walked back into her office with a smile on her face. "It' good to finally meet you, Mrs. Taylor."

'It's nice to meet you too, Dr. Westbrook. Please call me Linda."

"How are you doing today, Trey. I hope you've been sleeping better?" Dr. Westbrook knew she was in for a fight when Trey came in not feeling like talking.

"I've been sleeping better since Trevor has given me relaxation exercises."

"How are the headaches?"

"They were fine until I went to the crime scene the other day and still didn't remember anything."

"Trey, you have to stop forcing yourself to remember."

"How am I supposed to do that, Dr. Westbrook? The pressure is coming from all ends. I want to be here when my child is born not in a middle of a damn murder trial. We just found out our baby may come early which isn't a good thing."

"Sorry to hear about the baby, Trey. Maybe it's time for us to do something different." Trey was happy to hear this because that means Dr. Westbrook was ready to hypnotize him.

"Great, I'm so glad that you see that hypnosis may be my only option to get my memory back."

"No, Trey, I wasn't referring to hypnosis." Dr. Westbrook could see the crestfallen look on Trey's face.

"Then what are you talking about?" Trey asked.

"We've been avoiding this, but I think it's time to deal with your feelings about Sonya and her actions. Mrs. Taylor maybe you would like to wait in the lobby until we finish this session."

"No, that won't be necessary. Linda knows all about my relationship with Sonya and we can speak freely in front of her." For the remainder of the session Trey told Dr. Westbrook about his relationship with Sonya and how much she'd changed by the time he graduated from college. Leaving the office thirty minutes later, Trey told Malinda the only way he would have lunch with Trevor and TJ was if she went with them. He checked with her first to see if she was tired and after she said she wasn't they went to do a little shopping until it was time to meet his brothers. As they were leaving the baby boutique, Trey was surprised to run into Dawn. He hadn't seen her since her visit to his office.

"Good morning, Ms. Nicholson." Trey was polite, but had an uneasy feeling meeting her again.

"Good morning, Mr. Taylor, nice to see you again." The smile on Dawn's face seemed fake to Trey.

"This is my wife, Malinda. Malinda this is Dawn Nicholson the leasing manager for the condo." Trey didn't like the suspicious look on Malinda's face.

"Wait a minute, Mr. Taylor. I'm a little confused I thought your wife's name was Sonya." Dawn had a puzzle look on her face.

"No, what made you think such a thing?" Trey asked confused.

"Mr. Taylor this conversation is making me uneasy." Dawn said.

"I get that, but I need to know why you would think my wife's name was Sonya?"

"When you guys came to rent the condo that's what you told me." Dawn responded.

"There must be some kind of mistake." Trey was worried and confused. Dawn didn't mention anything about someone being with him when she came to his office.

"It was nice meeting you, Ms. Nicholson." Malinda ended their conversation and headed towards their car.

"Linda slow down." Trey had to trot to keep up with his wife.

"No, what I need to do is find out what the hell is going on, Trey. I want you to take me home right now." Malinda hadn't been this angry in a long time.

"Ok, I'll call Trevor and TJ to let them know we can't make it for lunch then we can go home and relax." Trey saw the hurt in his wife's eyes.

"I need to be alone, Trey. Go have lunch with your brothers."

"You know I can't leave you alone when you're this upset."

"That's exactly what I expect you to do. Carmen will be over around one o'clock, so I won't be alone for long."

"Ok, I tell you what. I will meet with my brothers for lunch once Carmen arrives. You can go upstairs to rest, and I'll stay downstairs until your sister arrives."

"Do what you want, Trey. Just take me home right now." Malinda and Trey was home twenty minutes later. Malinda went upstairs and slammed their bedroom door. Trey went into the family room to think about what happened with Dawn.

Trey canceled lunch with his brothers. Once Carmen arrived to stay with Malinda he headed straight to his parents' house. The more time passed the more disturbing the situation became. He tried to talk to Malinda before her sister arrived, but she didn't have anything to say to him. He told her to just say something to let him know she was okay. She told him to leave her alone. She wouldn't say anything else to him, so he left her alone. Arriving at his parents' house Trey found them in the family room.

"What's wrong, Trey?" Tanya didn't like the distressed look on her son's face.

"I've got to get my memory back before I lose my wife and child."

"What's wrong with, Malinda? I thought she believed in your innocence?" Trenton liked Malinda, but he wasn't going to stand by and let her worry his son.

72

"She does or did before we ran into the lady that said I rented the condo today. She said that I was with Sonya when I rented it and I told her that Sonya was my wife."

"What the hell. Did you guys do a background check on this woman? Why didn't she mention this when she was at your office?" Trenton asked.

"No, Dad. We didn't do a background check on her. I saw that the signature on the lease was mine and didn't take it any further. I didn't get a chance to ask her why she didn't mention it earlier, because Linda was upset. I had to tend to her." Trey explained to his parents.

"Well it's time to take it further. I'll be right back. Stay here and talk to your mom." Trenton left Trey and Tanya while he went to his study.

"Mom, I'm so scared for Malinda. She has never been this angry at me. I'm afraid this stress may send her into early labor."

"Lia and I will go visit her later when Lia gets off work. I guess that conversation was a lot to handle. I know she still believes in your innocence, Trey."

"CJ will be home tomorrow. I'm afraid he and their dad will gain up on her about leaving me until the trial is over."

"If she could handle the reporters, she'll be able to let her family know her place is with you, Trey. Stop making more of this then necessary."

"I don't know, Mom. You should have seen the look on her face when she got into the car after we talked to Dawn."

"Let's get together for brunch Sunday. We will arrange it so everyone can put their cards on the table." Tanya didn't get any further because Trenton came back into the room and said that he and Trey had a meeting with Victoria.

## Chapter Fourteen

Instead on going out for Sunday brunch the family decided to meet up at the Taylor's home. This was decided because of the nature of the meeting. Things were still strained between Trey and Malinda and didn't get any better when her brother came back to add his two cents into their relationship. Trey's been sleeping in the spare bedroom because that's the only way Malinda agreed to stay home. When CJ came home and found out about the condo he was just as angry as Malinda. Malinda had to keep the two men from getting into a physical fight. When CJ left, that is when Malinda told Trey she still needed space.

They had the food catered since no one was in the mood to cook. All of Trey's family was there even Talia's husband (Ronald Drake Ross). Jerome and his parents were there too along with Malinda's dad and brother. Carmen was with a friend because they didn't want her to be there for the discussion. Malinda's Aunt Maria wasn't there because they weren't speaking any longer after Maria went after her dad when Malinda's mom Marlene died. Malinda couldn't understand why she would disgrace her mom honor. She was kind of off today because she was having cramps. They were mild and nothing like the ones she had before when Talia took her to the hospital. Everyone was still gathered in the dining room after they finished eating and the cleaning was done to get the meeting started.

"Ok. I think it's time to address the elephant in the room. When Trey and Linda were out shopping the other day, they bumped into that Dawn girl that said Trey and Sonya rented the condo together." Trenton was ready to fight to the end for his son. He felt it was time to weed out the fools that didn't believe in Trey's innocence even Malinda.

"It seems to me that every day that passes more incriminating evidence is found against, Trey. We need to face the fact that maybe what the facts state are true." CJ said. Most of the people in the room including his sister look at him like he was crazy.

"That's your opinion and you're welcome to it. If there is anyone else that feels the same way as CJ it's time for you all to follow him out the door right now." Trenton wasn't playing when he said it was time to clean house.

"Sir, I don't mean any disrespect, but Linda has been through a lot and she doesn't need all this added stress." CJ decided it was time to tone it down a notch.

"If the pressure is too much for her to handle than maybe it's best for her to go home with you guys." Trenton wasn't backing down.

"Hold on a minute, Dad. CJ is speaking for himself not my wife." Trey didn't like the direction this meeting was taking.

"Then it's time for your wife to speak up and let the family know where she stands." Trenton said sternly. Tanya put a loving hand on his leg but that didn't stop his agenda.

"Dad, this isn't the forum for this conversation. That discussion should be private between me and my wife." Trey didn't realize his dad was going to pull something like this at the meeting.

"It's okay, Trey. Mr. Trenton my loyalty lies with my husband. I won't be leaving him or our home." Malinda looked at her dad and brother as she made her point clear.

"That takes care of that issue. Now, TJ and Lia where do you guys stand?" Trenton planned on getting everything and everyone out in the open.

"Dad, Trey and I have talked about this and we're good." Talia's said embarrassed to be called out. Ronald held her hand tightly for support.

"Dad, I don't feel like I should be called out because I had questions. You and I both know that evidence less than what Trey is up against have ended in convictions." TJ didn't want to be kicked around by the family because he thought Trey might be guilty.

"Don't talk to me about evidence, TJ. You're letting your petty jealousy against your brother color your judgment." Trenton was still pissed at TJ and Talia.

"Guys cut this out right now. We are supposed to come together to see what we can do to prove Trey's innocence not call each other out on our shortcomings." Tanya didn't like the way her husband was being so hardnosed.

"Trent, man you need to lighten up and let everyone express how they feel even if it's not what you want to hear." James Ward was Jerome's dad and Trenton's best friend.

"Jim, we don't have time for foolishness. Yes, Trey should've been proactive in Sonya's situation, but what's done is done. The trial is fast approaching, and we have to be prepared." Trenton continued.

"Jim is right, Trent. I'm sure no one in this room wants Trey to be guilty and just because we want to look out for Linda doesn't mean we're against Trey." Malinda's dad Corey took offense to Trenton's abrupt attitude.

"Dad are your people done with the background check on Dawn?" Trey wanted to get into a dialogue that would be beneficial.

"Yes. The report will be delivered to Victoria sometime today. We have a nine o'clock meeting with her in the morning."

"Well, since it seems everyone is getting restless and ready to go, I want to take a few minutes to share my thoughts." Tara listened as everyone had their say, but her feelings were the same as her dad's.

"Tara, you're not a cop so you should let them do their jobs." Talia was irritated that Tara always wanted to play the detective.

"I'm not trying to be a cop. I feel my job is more important than a cop's. Anyway, Rome and I been working on a few things. We had to target the people we know that wants Trey out of the way. We removed Greg Timmons off the list because he was and still is incarcerated. The main two suspects we're closing in on are closer to Linda than Trey: Malcolm and Maria."

"Tara how could you think my aunt would be involved in something like this?" Malinda didn't want to talk to her aunt any longer but didn't think she would hurt her.

"Your aunt is crazy and blames my brother for your cutting her out of your life." Tara responded.

"That may be true, but she wouldn't go this far to get even." Malinda insisted.

"Maybe we should think about this, sis. That woman got some wicket things going on inside her head." Malinda looked at her brother like he was crazy. She missed her aunt and was close to her after her mom die until she made the moves on her dad. She didn't want to believe her aunt would seek revenge that would hurt her.

"CJ's right. You know I don't like that woman and with good reasons. I wouldn't put anything past her." Trey thought it was time to look at Maria from a different viewpoint.

"Wait a minute. I have two more names for you guys. Chris and Sonya Young." Tara added.

"Now you're going way out there, Tara." Talia was getting sick of her baby sister.

"Wow, I think you're on to something, baby sis." Everyone in the room was shocked when TJ made that statement.

"What are you talking about, TJ?" This time it was Malinda inquiring to TJ.

"What if Chris lied about knowing Sonya's condition and she convinced him to devise this plan to get even with Trey? We know she could talk her dad into anything."

"I don't see it, TJ. That means he would have to look his wife in the face every day knowing he was keeping that big secret from her." Tanya couldn't believe he would be that cruel to his wife. She knew Trenton better not treat her in that manner.

"We have a grieving dad that's helpless to do anything about his daughter's condition and a vindictive woman that can get even with a man she wanted for years but failed to get him back." TJ was finally getting the picture that Trey may be innocent.

"Trey, since Sharon reached out to you maybe it's time for you to do the same. Try to see if she had any idea Sonya was dying or if she believed her husband knew." Trenton knew this was kind of cold blooded, but he wanted to do whatever it takes to clear his son's name.

"Dad, I don't think that's a good idea. She is really suffering right now. If Mr. Chris kept this from her, she's going to be even more devastated. I don't want to add to her pain." Trey liked both of Sonya's parents even though Chris had come to detest Trey.

"We've covered a lot of ground today. Honey, I think we should let everyone get on with their day." Tanya was tired and ready to spend some time alone with her family. They conversed for another half hour then everyone left to continue with their day.

## Chapter Fifteen

Trey wondered why it was so dark and felt like he was floating. He was trying to figure out what was wrong with him and why he felt so sluggish. He looked around to see if there was anything familiar about his surroundings, but he didn't recognize anything. He heard voices that were far away but getting closer. He didn't recognize the voices maybe because his head was hurting so badly. Then he saw her standing in front of him looking like an angel. Why would her image taunt him? He didn't know because even though she looks like an angel all the sudden horns started to point out of her head. Then her face started to become distorted. Trey was so fearful of the image in front of him he tried to run, but then he noticed his hands and legs were bound. Now struggling and shouting leave me alone the next thing he knew was Malinda shaking him awake.

"Trey are you ok?" Malinda looked at Trey like he had lost his mind.

"Me, is the baby ok? Why are you shouting at me, baby?" Trey didn't know what was wrong with Malinda, but he was worried about her.

"I'm fine, Trey and so is the baby, but the way you were shouting I don't know about you."

"What time is it baby?" Trey asked.

"Almost seven o'clock. Why won't you answer my question, Trey?"

"I have to get ready to meet dad and Victoria. Is Carmen here?"

"Yes, Trey. She came over last night after you went to bed."

"Good. I'll be home as soon as I can." Trey jumped out of bed and headed for the bathroom to take his shower.

Victoria was never so happy to have a meeting start. The case seemed to hit a roadblock until all the sudden gold was dropped into their laps. She had to admit that when former Judge Trenton Aaron Taylor wants something, he gets it. She didn't know how he was able to get Judge Melvin Winston off the case, but he did and hiring that private investigator was a stroke of genius. The judge and Trey would be there in a few minutes, so she had to act like this news wasn't as important as it really was because she didn't want to get Trey's hopes up. What they needed was for Trey to get his memory back, so he could shed light on what happened on that faithful day. The buzzer from her assistant brought Victoria out of her daydream. She was excited when she told her that the Taylors were there. Once Trenton and Trey were seated in front of her, Victoria made small talk.

"How was your weekend, Trey?"

"It would have been better if I gotten my memory back."

"That will come in due time. Is there anything new you guys want to share with me?" Victoria listened as Trenton and Trey told her about what happened at the family brunch. This was like icing on the cake for her.

"Are you guys ready for some good news?" Trenton and Trey faces brighten up.

"Yes, it's long overdue, Tori." Trey couldn't wait to hear what Victoria had to tell them.

"I have the report from the private investigator that checked out Dawn Nicholson."

"That's what I'm talking about, results. Don't keep us in suspense, Victoria?" Trenton said.

"Dawn Nicholson, the leasing agent doesn't exist." Victoria said in excitement.

"What do you mean she doesn't exist, Tori?" Victoria wasn't making sense to Trey. He had talked to Dawn on several occasions.

"It has been proven that Dawn Nicholson is really a bank teller named, Joanna Lynn Dawson. She is none other than a close friend to the one and only Malcolm Jayden Winston." Victoria said proudly.

"This doesn't make sense to me, Tori." Trey was so tired of saying these words but didn't have anything better to say.

"The first thing we need to do is to have that condo lease examined by a handwriting expert."

"I see where you're going with this, Victoria. Trey may not have signed the leased to that condo."

"That's right. The prosecutor is relying on this identification by Joanna to seal his case." Trenton added.

"Wow, I guess that's why Malcolm called to harass me. It seemed he would have been better off leaving me alone so he wouldn't become suspect." All kinds of thoughts were going through Trey's mind.

"I think it's time to dig deeper into some of the theories Tara brought up at the meeting." Trenton felt blessed to have such intelligent children. He just wished he could get TJ and Trey on the same page. Trey still didn't want his oldest brother anywhere near his case even though TJ seemed to be coming around.

"That's true we should, but I have ordered a detailed investigation on Malcolm Winston. I have a gut feeling that there are more people involved in framing you." Victoria was determined to cover all of their bases.

"While you're at it, I hope you did the same for Chris Young and Maria Dixon. We should add Gregory Timmons to the list; even though he was incarcerated he still could have been a part of the plan to frame my son."

"What's bothering me is that if Mr. Chris had something to do with this plan and kept it from his wife, she'll be destroyed all over again."

"We can't worry about that right now, Trey. I know that may sound cold, but we have to get down and dirty to get you out of this mess." Trenton had a one-track mind.

"Guys, I have a few more tricks up my sleeve so let's table this for now. You all can go home to your families. Trey you need to prepare Malinda for the possibility that her aunt is involved."

"I know. This is really going to hurt her if she is involved. The two of them used to be so close, now Linda won't talk to her at all. Of course, Maria blames me, but she needs to look in the mirror. How does she expect Linda to feel when her aunt is trying to become her stepmom?"

"Again, I say we can't worry about that right now, Trey." Trenton was getting tired of these minor problems impeding on how they prepared the case.

"Dad, I'm going to have you to drop me off at the office, so I can do more brainstorming with Tara and JW. I'll have one of them take me back home after we're done."

"Gentlemen, I'll keep you posted. Trey, I want you to rest. Also, don't give Dr. Westbrook any problems at your session tomorrow."

"What makes you think I'm giving her problems, Tori?"

"I know you think she's not doing her job since you don't have your memory back, but she's an expert in her field so let her work her magic."

"On that note, Dad, I think we better get a move on before you land in the doghouse with mom for not spending enough time with her while she's on vacation."

"Do I look like a man that is led by the nose by a woman? Never mind don't answer that." Trey and Trenton left Victoria's office feeling better about the case.

Malinda was at her dad's house talking with her brother CJ. He was still pissed about the way the conversation went at the meeting held at Trey's parents' house. He felt that Trenton was rude and disrespectful. It took her a while to calm him down. She told him he shouldn't be talking like that with Carmen in the house even though she was glued upstairs in her bedroom with a couple of her friends. She sympathized with CJ because she told Trey the same thing that both his dad and sister Tara was rude when it came to his case. Trey tried to make excuses for them, but they needed to chill out. Malinda was thrown off guard when CJ asked her if she believed Trey was having an affair with Sonya.

"Of course, he wasn't having an affair with that crazy heifer. I trust my husband not to hurt me like that and furthermore after all the bullshit she took us through he wouldn't look twice at her." Malinda had an attitude with CJ because she needed his support right now.

"Calm down, Linda. I just asked you a simple question dang. It's just she had to be really crazy to keep chasing after a man that wasn't interested." CJ explained.

"We'll, she was, CJ..." Before Malinda could finish what, she was saying, the front door opened. Then her dad and aunt walked in.

"Oh, hell no. I know you're not bringing this hussy around my baby sister?" CJ stood and approached his dad and aunt.

"Keep your voice down, CJ. You do realize that you're in my house, don't you?" Corey Sr. said not realizing what CJ was talking about.

"I know that, Dad, but you know it's not a good idea to bring her around Carmen." CJ said pointing at Maria.

"I do know that. Since Carmen isn't here that's not a problem."

"Wrong, she's upstairs with two of her friends. They decided to have the sleepover here instead of her friend's house." CJ was given his aunt an evil eye while talking to his dad.

"Shit, Maria go wait in the car for me while I go check on Carmen." Corey said.

Maria moved, but not towards the door, but towards Malinda. She stepped back a little when CJ jumped in front of her. "Get out of my way, CJ." Maria said.

"Have you lost your mind? You're not going anywhere near my sister." CJ yelled at his aunt.

"CJ don't make a scene. Maria, I said go wait in the car." This time his dad's voice was sterner.

"I just want a few minutes to talk to my niece, Corey. Mindy, please talk to me." Maria begged.

"She has nothing to say to you. Now get the hell out before Carmen finds out you're here." CJ was getting madder by the minute.

"You people are a trip. I just want to talk to your spoiled ass for a minute, Mindy." Maria was losing patience with trying to get back in good graces with her oldest niece.

"Don't call me that. I have nothing to say to you, lady." Malinda stood and was shocked to see that blood was running down her leg. Everyone in the room seemed to panic. Hearing the noise Carmen came downstairs followed by her two friends. The first-person Carmen noticed was Maria. She headed towards her aunt ready to give her a piece of her mind until she saw what was going on with Malinda. Carmen ran upstairs at full speed to get her cell phone. She was upset when Trey didn't answer. Going over to Malinda when she came back downstairs tears began to roll down her face. Once the EMS took Malinda away with CJ riding with them, Carmen told her friends they needed to go home so she could go to the hospital to be with her sister.

## Chapter Sixteen

Trey was sleeping in a chair next to the bed of his wife who had gone through an emergency C-Section yesterday for the birth of their son. It had been a rough night for both families. He would never forget the frantic call he received yesterday from his young sister-in-law about what happened at the Robert's house. She begged him to stop by to get her, but all that was on Trey's mind was getting to the hospital to be with his wife. Trey told Carmen he would send Beverly to pick her up. He was so damn mad he hoped that his wife wouldn't notice. What the hell was that train wreck doing talking to his wife. From what his mom told him Malinda's problem wasn't caused by Maria, but Trey didn't want to hear that.

Once he arrived at the hospital, he didn't give Jerome a chance to stop the truck completely before he jumped out and ran into the emergency room. He was glad to see his parents there. His mom told him Talia was working so she was able to go into the room with Malinda until he got there. Seeing CJ and Corey didn't make Trey happy at all. Trey shot an evil glance at both men before he followed the nurse to take him back to see Malinda. When he arrived at the labor room Talia came out followed by the doctor explaining that they were going to have to do an emergency C-Section on Malinda once Trey completed the paperwork. Trey didn't want to fill out paperwork. All he wanted was to be with his wife. Talia explained that it was necessary, so they could treat Malinda as soon as possible. Hearing Malinda moan brought Trey back to the present.

"Baby, I'm right here try to take it easy." Malinda had been given a sedative once the baby was born because she began to begin to hemorrhage. They had to go in twice to stop the bleeding and when they went in the second time, they had to give her a hysterectomy. When they told her the extent of her condition, Malinda became hysterical. Now waking up for the first time she was groggy.

"What happened to me, Trey?" Malinda spoke so softly Trey had to bend his head closer, so he could hear her.

"How much do you remember, baby?" Trey didn't want to tell her too much too soon.

"I was rushed to the hospital." Malinda stopped and felt her stomach and began to panic.

"Calm down baby."

"Where's our baby, Trey?"

"Linda, it's okay he's fine."

"You said he."

"Yes, we have a son, Linda." Trey was glad to see the big smile on Malinda's face until she remembered the rest.

"Wait a minute, Trey. What else happened?" Malinda had a strange look on her face like she was trying to remember. Trey knew that look because he's had it for weeks now. Taking Malinda's hand Trey begin to explain about the surgery. It broke his heart as silent tears dropped from Malinda's eyes knowing she could never have another baby.

"What about our son, Trey? Is he going to be alright? I want to see him, Trey."

"Not right now because he's small and needs time to get stronger."

"I want to see my baby, Trey." Malinda insisted.

"I have to check with the doctor. Your family is waiting to see you and so is mine."

"I need to see my baby first, Trey. I need to know he's going to be ok." Malinda started to cry and as Trey was comforting her CJ and Carmen walked into the room.

"Are you ok, Linda?" Carmen sounded like a wounded child who lost her favorite toy.

"Hi, baby girl. Come give your big sister a hug." Malinda knew she had to be strong for her baby sister.

"You have one of those for me, sis?" CJ was uncomfortable in this situation. He didn't like how pale his sister looked.

"Of course, get over here, boy." Trey was glad that Malinda seemed to change her mood for her siblings. She was back in control of her emotions.

"Dad is waiting to see you too, Linda." CJ knew Malinda was still upset with their dad for bringing Maria to the house.

"Too bad, I want to see my baby." Malinda turned to Trey after she made that statement.

"I'll go check to see what the doctor has to say about that, baby." After Trey left the room both CJ and Malinda were surprised at Carmen's outburst.

"I hate her. Every time she comes around something bad happens."

"Carmen this wasn't Aunt Maria's fault. I've been having problems this entire pregnancy." Malinda felt the say way as Carmen, but she didn't want to add more fuel to the fire.

"The old man has to see how much this upset the family. Why the hell does he keep bringing her around?" CJ was still pissed with their dad.

"In his defense he didn't think neither one of you guys would be at home." Malinda didn't want all three of them to be mad with their dad at the same time.

"Let's talk about something positive. What are you guys going to name your son?" CJ wanted to get that sad look off Malinda's face.

"I don't know if Trey wants him to be a junior or not. Our deal was if it was a boy, he names him, and I would name the girl."

"We're going to leave now so you can rest, Linda. I'm sure Trey will be back in a little while. Don't let that lady's visit take anything else from you." CJ said as he and Carmen gave Malinda a hug then left the room in search of their dad.

When Trey arrived at the nursery, Talia was in there with the doctor and another nurse. His mom had to leave to take his dad to his doctor's appointment. Of course, his dad gave her a hard time stating that it was too much going on to waste time with that quack. Trey couldn't let Malinda know how worried he was about their son. He only weighed three pounds and four ounces, and his lungs weren't fully developed. He prayed that their son would survive because Malinda would lose it if he didn't make it. Once he got Talia's attention, she came out to talk to him.

"How's he doing, Lia?" Trey asked.

"He has a lot going against him, Trey. With his lungs underdeveloped he's at risk for infection." Talia was so tired, but she wanted to do all she could for her nephew.

"Linda is anxious to see him."

"I know she is, Trey, but they're not going to allow visitors inside for a little while. I can check to see if it's okay with her doctor if you could bring her here and she could see him from the window." Talia knew her doctor probably won't let Malinda visit until tomorrow.

"Whatever you could do would be appreciated. She's hanging on by a thread. When I left her CJ and Carmen was there. She doesn't want to see her dad."

"I heard about what happened, but the visit wasn't the cause for her early delivery, the placenta separated."

"I know that, but what was he thinking bringing that woman around the family." Trey said angrily.

"From what CJ said they weren't supposed to be there, so I guess he thought he was sneaking her in."

"Do you have time to go with me to see Linda? I know you would be able to explain better why we can't see the baby right now."

"Sure, you can go back to her room. I'll be there in five or ten minutes." Trey hugged and thanked his sister and headed back to his wife.

The plan was getting out of hand. Why did all of this have to happen now? He had to pay and pay dearly for all the shit he put everyone through. Rich people think they could get away with anything and think the world owed them something. Here he was walking around pretending he couldn't remember what happen that day, but that's just a load of bull. The trial will be starting soon, and he will finally get what he deserves. Even after he's locked up that's not going to be the end of it. He still had more suffering he had to do before the end of his miserable life.

There have been a few delays, but that's to be expected. Now was the time to make a move since the stakes were higher. Getting everyone back on the same page hasn't been easy, but after putting the fear of God in them, they had to shape up. The next phase will be more dramatic and lasting. It's so good when you see all your hard work come together. Sometimes it was difficult dealing with others, but in this case, it wasn't a one-person job so that's the price to pay for dealing with weak people. Everything was working out just fine even with the minor setbacks. Now it was time to sit back and reap the rewards.

## Chapter Seventeen

It had been a few rough days for Trey and Malinda. Early Friday morning, Trey was sitting in Dr. Westbrook's office waiting on her to come in. Trey was with Trevor. He was shocked when TJ called him last night to see how he and Malinda was doing, checked on the baby, and to see if Trey wanted him to go to his appointment with Dr. Westbrook today. Trey would acknowledge that he seemed to be trying, but something in his gut told him not to trust his oldest brother. When Trey told Trevor how he felt, Trevor told him to be open minded, but if he felt strongly not to trust their brother than that's what he should go with.

Malinda was still in the hospital but was expected to be released on Monday. Trey had a feeling she wasn't trying to get better, so she could stay near their son. They still hadn't picked out a name for the baby, but Trey decided he didn't want his son to be a junior, so he told Malinda after his appointment today they will decide. Baby boy Taylor wasn't what they wanted their son to be referred to any longer. The little guy was getting stronger every day, but still wasn't out of the woods. He had gained a few ounces since his birth, but Malinda was devastated when she saw him for the first time yesterday. She later asked Trey how something that little had a fighting chance.

Trey had to laugh at himself while he waited on Dr. Westbrook. He and Malinda made an interesting couple right now with his memory loss and her slight depression. He also had to laugh at his dad because he supported Trey completely, but he didn't want to come to any of his counseling sessions. He said he gets enough of doctors dealing with his primary and cardiologist not to mention Tanya and Talia who was always on him about his health and diet. Trey looked at Dr. Westbrook and smiled as she rushed into the room.

"Sorry to keep you guys waiting. It seems like every time you have an appointment with me a minor unexpected crisis happens."

"Don't worry about it. I was hoping we don't use up the entire hour, so I could get back to my wife and son."

"Oh my God. Your wife had the baby. I thought she wasn't due for another six weeks?"

"She wasn't, she had to have an emergency C-Section on Tuesday, that's why I cancelled my session."

"Well congratulations, how are mother and son doing?"

"They're still in the hospital. Malinda is expected to be released on Monday, but it will be a while before the baby is released since he only weighed a little over three pounds at birth."

"I'm so sorry to hear that, Trey. I will keep all of you guys in my prayers. How have you been handling all of the pressure in your life?"

"As best as I could. I don't have my memory back, but there has been some good news as far as my case is concerned."

"That's something to be happy about. I have some good news for you too. Since your treatments haven't been going as planned on your next visit if you don't have any flashes of memory, we will try hypnosis."

"Wow, I didn't expect to hear that from you. The first time it wasn't on my mind you bring it up as an option." Trey responded.

"Trevor have you noticed any changes in Trey's behavior since you been working with him?" Dr. Westbrook didn't want to have to do the hypnosis, but it's been almost a month, so other actions were needed since Trey's trial was near.

"Trey was more relaxed before all this happened with Linda. I think he witnessed something horrifying so he is blocking out that painful memory." Trevor explained.

"We're on the same track. Trey you haven't had even flashes of memories?"

"No, to tell you the truth, I'm afraid to sleep sometimes after that bad dream I had of Sonya. Now with the baby and Malinda I have more important things to worry about."

"Ok, this is what I need you to do between now and your next appointment. Take time to meditate. Try to free your mind from everything in a dark room if possible. You may find that once you are totally relaxed it may open up your mind to what you're blocking out."

"Sure thing. I'll try to do that before I bring Linda home. I'll have a lot of help with her because my family and hers said they would help out." After giving Trey a few samples of light sedatives, Trey and Trevor left the office to go to the hospital to see Malinda and the baby.

Trevor dropped Trey off at the hospital and told him he would be back in a few hours after he's taken care of a few appointments. Trey was feeling pretty good about his session with Dr. Westbrook. He felt that he will be getting his memory back soon and all of this would be a distant memory. So, wrapped up in his thoughts, Trey didn't notice Malinda's dad coming towards him.

"Good morning, Trey." Corey used his professor voice he used on students to get their attention.

"Morning, Mr. Cory. How are you doing today?" Trey knew that Corey wanted to see Malinda, but she still refused to see him."

"This has gone on long enough. I want to see my daughter right now."

"I'm sorry, Mr. Corey. CJ and I have been trying to talk her into seeing you, but she's still a little upset by what happened at your house the day our son was born."

"That was an unfortunate occurrence. No one was supposed to be at my house."

"I understand that, and Malinda knows that our baby's early birth wasn't the cause of that scene, but she feels that you are totally disregarding your family by having a relationship with Ms. Maria."

"Well that's not the case and I've tried to explain that to them on many occasions."

"Sir, they understand you need to move on with your life, but not with a woman they consider a gold-digger and disrespectful to their mom's memory." Trey went over this before with Corey, but nothing had changed.

"I'm a grown man with a deceased wife. I have a right to move on with my life with anyone that makes me happy." Corey was getting irritated with Trey and his family telling him whom he shouldn't date.

"I'll go back there to see if I could get Linda to change her mind and will let you know, sir." Trey left Corey in the hospital lobby and headed up to see Malinda. He couldn't wait to tell his wife about his session. He felt sorry for her dad, so the first order of business was to see if she would see him even if it was just for a few minutes. When he arrived to her room, she was resting in her bed talking to Tanya and Talia. After giving them a brief hug, Trey went to sit by his wife's side.

"Baby your dad is waiting to see you in the lobby."

"I'm not up for this, Trey. All I can think about is our son. I hope you don't mind your mom and sister been working on a list of names with me."

"No, I don't mind, baby, but I think you should see your dad because he is really worried about you."

"Linda, Trey is right. This is a time for family to stick together. You need your dad right now so don't push him away." Talia hoped her friend would change her mind about seeing her dad. They were so close until he started dating Maria.

"Lia, it's not fair for you guys to gain up on me. I need to pick out my son's name and rest, so I can see him when the doctor says it's ok."

"Stop this mess right now, Linda. I've sat here with my mouth closed and watched and listened to you young folks communicate, and I must say I'm saddened. Your dad loves and needs you right now. I'm sure there are things you have done in your life that he doesn't like, but he didn't cut you off. It's time for you to grow up and accept life isn't going to go the way you want it to all the time. Now I'm going to get your dad and I expect you to treat him with the respect he deserves." Tanya said then left the room to go get Corey Sr.

"I guess my choice was taken away from me." Malinda said sadly.

"Baby, he doesn't have to stay long just hear him out."

"I will, but not for long. I want to rest. How did your session go, Trey?"

"The gist of it, I have homework to do some relaxation exercises and if I don't get my memory or flashes of it, Dr. Westbrook will do hypnosis on my next visit."

"Why do you sound like this is something you don't want, Trey? You've been pressuring her to do this from the beginning." Talia didn't understand why Trey didn't sound happy.

"It's just so much going on right now. With Linda coming home on Monday, I was thinking about skipping my session since they don't seem to be working anyway."

"You don't have to worry about me, honey. Lia, your mom, CJ, and Carmen will see to it I'm settled in. I even heard from Tara and she offered to help." Malinda was surprised when Tara offered to help. She knew Tara was doing it for Trey and her nephew.

"Well, I have to head back to work. Enjoy your visit with your dad and let the nurse know if you need me for anything." Talia gave Trey and Malinda a slight hug then left the room.

## Chapter Eighteen

There was a house full of people at Trey and Malinda's on Monday when Malinda was released from the hospital. Trey was sad, and Malinda cried all the way home because they couldn't bring their son home. The good news was he was getting stronger every day, but they knew it would be weeks before he was able to come home. Tanya promised to make sure he was given the best of care now that she was back to work. Trey didn't want to leave his wife, but he and his dad had an appointment with Victoria to go over the witness list and a few other details. They were hoping that she would have news regarding the other background checks.

When Trey and Trenton arrived at Victoria's office, she wasn't there. She was tied up in court but told her assistant to tell the men she would be there in fifteen minutes. While they waited in the lobby, Trey and his dad talked about their weekend. Trey visited the baby and Malinda only for a few hours on Sunday because he wanted to get home to prepare for the homecoming and to do the exercises and meditation. He also skipped dinner with his parents which was probably a good thing since TJ was there. Coming out of his daydream when he heard his dad repeatedly call his name, Trey didn't realize he had zoned out.

"Sorry, Dad. What were you saying?"

"Your mom and I missed you at dinner yesterday."

"It was for the best because I was so frustrated that no matter what I try nothing is making me remember what happened that day."

"Well let's hope tomorrow's session will give us the help we need to clear your name. How's business?" Trenton asked.

"I guess we're lucky that we're not losing clients, but on the other hand we're haven't had an increase neither." Trey answered.

Victoria rushed into the lobby and told them to follow her into her office. On the way there she stopped and laid a stack of files on her assistant's desk.

"How are you guys doing today? Just give me a few minutes to get myself together." Victoria laid everything else she had in her hands on her desk then told Trey and Trenton to have a seat.

"Okay, today my co-counsel will be joining us to give a status report on the background checks we have underway. I've prepared the witness list for you guys to review. Let me know if you would like anyone else called or if any of the witnesses on the list will be a problem." Victoria handed a list to Trey and Trenton and gave them a few minutes to review it. She also told them when Reuben joined them, he would have a list of the prosecution witnesses.

"Why are you calling Ms. Sharon as a witness, Tori?" Trey frowned at this because he didn't see the point of calling Sonya's mom to the stand.

"She could be used as a circumstantial witness." Victoria responded.

"I don't see how when she's the mother of the deceased, Victoria?" Trenton didn't understand what strategy Victoria was trying to use.

"Think about it, Trenton, if she thought Trey killed her daughter would she have paid him a visit?

"I guess not, but she won't go against her husband to testify for us. Using her as a hostile witness would only hurt our case."

"We won't push the issue. It was just a thought. We'll use Dr. Westbrook as an expert witness as well as an associate of mine that is a ballistic expert." Just as Victoria finished her statement Reuben walked into her office. She introduced him again to Trenton and Trey. Reuben got right down to business sitting on the outside edge of the desk to the left of Victoria.

"Ok, we'll start off with the easiest person in the investigation Greg Timmons. We can count him out because not only was he incarcerated, but he was also in solitary confinement."

"We figured as much, but it didn't hurt to check." Trenton was glad they were able to cross one suspect off their list. The one-hour Greg was allowed out of his cell he wouldn't have any phone privileges.

"Next, we have Chris Young. His profile is interesting because I can't say he lied to the police, but he definitely lied to his wife because he knew Sonya was dying."

"Oh my God. How could he keep something like that from Ms. Sharon?" All the sudden Trey had a terrible headache.

"Are you ok, son?" Trenton asked.

"No, all of the sudden a sharp pain went through my head." Trey sat in his seat next to his dad rubbing his temples for about five minutes before they were able to continue. Victoria had her assistant to bring in water, so Trey could take his medicine.

Reuben continued with his report once Trey was settled. "Young went to all of Sonya's appointments with her and was there when she was first diagnosed. From the information I gathered he was part of Sonya's decision not to have treatment since the cancer was already at Stage 4."

"This shines a new light on the dynamics of the case." Trenton knew how devoted Chris was to his daughter and if she wanted to make a last-ditch effort to destroy Trey's life, he would have been right by her side.

"Yes, it does because they were thick as thieves during her last days. He even took time off from work. Next, we have Maria Dixon. She's a slippery one, but there seems to be a connection between her and Malcolm Winston."

"What makes you say that, Reuben?" Trey didn't want Malinda's family to be involved in this mess, but he knew that Maria was upset with him about the distance Malinda keeps between she and Maria.

97

"There have been sightings between Maria and Malcolm. The only thing is these sightings were few and far between so it's difficult to say they weren't chance meetings."

"I wasn't going to go that route, but maybe it's time for JW to use his computer skills to track our suspects' whereabouts over the last few months." Trey knew he didn't have to explain exactly what kind of tracking Jerome would be doing.

"Son, I'm one step ahead of you. Jerome and Tara are doing what they must do to get the information we need. We knew you were too emotionally attached to go hard like we need to." Trenton said.

"Dad what are you having them doing?" Trey asked.

"What we've been talking about today. We can't wait on the police or the court system to do anything because they feel they have you dead to rights, so they're not looking for any other suspects."

"Trey, your dad is right. We need to take the gloves off. The trial will be starting soon and if we had to go in there with what we have right now, you're be sure to get twenty-five to life." This was the first time Victoria had spoken up in a while.

"Why are you guys under the impression that I'm not ready to fight hard. I need to be around for my wife and son. That's why I've been working so hard to get my memory back. I thought the training I've been doing with Trevor would help, but everything is still a blank. I just hope tomorrow's session would bear some fruit."

"We're not saying you're not willing to fight hard, Trey but look how protective you are of Sharon. I feel bad for her too, but my number one concern is you." Trey looked at his dad with a blank expression on his face. His head was still hurting even though he had taken his medication long enough for it to have worked.

"So, the only other person left on our list is Dawn/Joanna. What did you find out about her?" Trey wanted to end this discussion, so he could go home and rest before he and Malinda went to see the baby whom they decided to name Tyrell Aston Taylor.

"I have to do more digging on her, but from what I've gathered so far she has been dating Malcolm for over a year. I guess he was able to hide his feelings for your wife for a while, but he became out of control and Joanna tried to break it off from him. For some reason the breakup didn't happen." Reuben explained.

"If that's all guys, I better head home to check on Linda?" Trey didn't want to let Victoria and Reuben know how bad his head was hurting.

"That's it for now. You guys have a good day. We'll be in touch soon." Victoria walked Trey and Trenton to the front door and headed back to her office to wrap things up with Reuben.

## Chapter Nineteen

Sharon was sitting in her kitchen on a bright and sunny Tuesday morning waiting on her husband to finish his shower and get dressed. He has been distant lately and didn't want to talk about anything but the upcoming trial. The last time they talked about the trial he liked to have bitten, her head off when she suggested that Trey may not be guilty. Chris said more than once that Trey murdered their daughter a long time ago by the way he treated her. Sharon didn't want to go against her husband, but she felt in her heart that Trey didn't do it and wanted the police to look at other suspects. Carl told her the DA was set on prosecuting Trey and refused to reopen the investigation. Sharon felt this was a big mistake and told Carl they had the wrong person on trial. Of course, she didn't say this in front of Chris because she didn't want to start another argument.

Sharon couldn't believe the call she received from one of Sonya's friends. This friend stated that she and Sonya stopped talking because she wouldn't help her in her plot to destroy Trey's life. That didn't matter too much to Sharon until this friend mentioned how sorry she was about Sonya's diagnosis and she was proud how Mr. Chris was handling everything. When she asked her to further explain the woman clammed up and said she had to answer another call. Sharon was planning on talking to Chris about the call as soon as he came downstairs. She was getting a creepy feeling from that call. Chris walked into the kitchen looking refreshed and relaxed.

"Our day is slowly approaching, Shar. The trial is less than three weeks away. That monster will finally get what he deserves for mistreating our daughter." Chris said proudly.

"Chris, we need to talk." Sharon didn't want to hear him go on and on about the case.

"Isn't that what we're doing?"

"Yes, but I mean we need to have a serious talk about Sonya's diagnosis."

"What about it?"

"When did you find out she was dying, Chris?"

"The same day you did when Carl came over."

"Chris, I need you to look at me when you say that please."

"Woman what's your problem?"

"You're my problem, Chris. Why are you keeping important information from me? I'll ask you again. When did you find out about Sonya's illness?"

"Why are you yelling? I told you when I found out about Sonya."

"So, you're going to continue to sit there and lie to my face, Chris?

"Stop accusing me of lying to you, Shar."

"Chris, you knew about Sonya's illness before Carl came to tell us the news."

"Why would you say a thing like that?"

"Because it's true. Now tell me when you found out?" Sharon was so mad at her husband. All the life seemed to go out of Chris when he replied.

"Almost three months ago." Chris said.

"Oh my God, Chris. How could you guys keep something like that from me?"

"Baby, Sonya didn't want to worry you."

"Don't you dare baby me, Chris. You know damn well I should've been told."

"It was Sonya's decision. I tried to convince her to tell you." Chris knew Sharon wasn't going to buy that.

"What else are you keeping from me, Chris?" Sharon asked.

"Listen, it's not my fault our daughter confided in me and not you." Chris said with an attitude.

"Oh, so we're going to make this a contest."

"No, I'm just saying that Sonya was devastated when she received the news. She begged me not to tell anyone including you."

"You thought her decision was okay. Both of us should've been there to support her not just you?"

"I have to go before I'm late for work."

"You're going to work, Chris?"

"Yes, I feel it's time for me to take my life back."

"Have a nice day, Chris." Sharon decided to give up. She knew Chris was lying to her, but she needed time alone to deal with what was on her mind. After Chris left, Sharon went upstairs to think about her next move.

Trey had mixed feelings about Malinda going with him to his therapy session. He would have preferred Trevor or Tara to come with him since Malinda should be at home resting. Their plans were to go see the baby after his session. The little guy was getting bigger every day but was still small and fragile. Trey just wanted his son to be okay and didn't mind letting Malinda and Talia name him. Malinda was especially upset with the fear that Tyrell wouldn't make it. If that happened, she would never know what it means to be a biological mother. They decided to call their son Ty for short. Malinda was getting along better with her dad, but he knew not to bring Maria's name up around his children. This made Trey happy because he knew how much she loved her dad. The next few minutes were intense for Trey because when Dr. Westbrook started the session today, she will be hypnotizing him.

Trey studied the information over the weekend and last night that Dr. Westbrook gave him at his last session about what happens to the brain during hypnosis. She explained that she felt his memory loss was connected to the painful headaches because there were things that happened that day that were too painful for him to remember. The information also explained while he was in the hypnotic state he will appear to be zoned-out. That was another reason he didn't want Malinda to be there in case he tripped out. The information said the most important thing to remember is the objective of the hypnosis is to release suppressed memories. Dr. Westbrook told Trey they will have to try to determine if his pain was due to the painful incident or the concussion he suffered. Dr. Westbrook walked into her office and greeted Trey and Malinda.

"Good to see you again, Linda. You're looking good. How is the baby?"

"He's getting bigger every day. We named him Tyrell Ashton Taylor." Malinda replied.

"Good strong name. Trey how are you feeling?"

"My head still hurts from time to time, but we're making progress on the case so that's a little relief on that front."

"Were you able to read the materials I gave to you at our last session?"

"Yes, I read everything, but I'm still a little unsettled about the outcome."

"That's to be expected. I need to let you know a few things before we begin. If at any time I feel this is too traumatic for you, I'll bring you out. You also need to understand it may take more than one time to see results. You'll have complete control of yourself and will be able to block out inputs from your senses. Do either of you have any questions before we get started?"

"No, we just want to get this over with, so we can go see Ty." Trey was ready to get out of there as soon as possible.

"Ok, I need you to go over to the chair next to the loveseat. If you don't mind Malinda could you stay seated here until we're done? I'll turn down the lights and you can start your breathing lesson, Trey." When Trey seemed relaxed, Dr. Westbrook went to sit in front of him on the loveseat. I need you to relax and free everything from your mind. I only want you to listen to the sound of my voice." Dr. Westbrook didn't use anything to induce Trey outside of the peaceful music she played. Trey was now relaxed and in a trance like state.

"Trey, I need you to take a moment and think back to the last time you had contact with Sonya Young. How did you start your day off?"

"I got to the office early. I wanted to get a few things done so I wouldn't have to be there long, so I could get back home to Linda." Trey felt at peace and like he didn't have a care in the world.

"What did you do once you entered the office?"

"I checked the schedule. I was about to record notes for Bev to transcribe."

"Ok you're doing good, Trey. What happened next?"

"I received a call."

"Good, who was the call from, Trey?"

Suddenly Trey began to become agitated. "Leave me alone."

"Trey, who do you want to leave you alone?"

"I said I don't have anything to say to you." Trey was getting upset and moving around in his chair.

"Trey, who was on the other end of the phone?"

"Sir, are you ok?" Trey was shifting around in the chair like he was uncomfortable.

"Trey, who is on the other end of the phone?"

"I don't understand, sir. Are you ok?"

"Trey, what's happening? Who is on the other end of the phone?" Dr. Westbrook didn't like how upset Trey was becoming.

"Please stop just stop." Trey was at a point where Dr. Westbrook knew she had to bring him back.

"Listen, to me, Trey. I'm going to count to three. When I get to three you will wake up refreshed. One, you're relaxed now take a deep breath, two, you're going to slowly open your eyes, and three you're fully awake."

"That was another dead end wasn't it?" Trey moved his head from side to side and realized he was pain free.

"I had to bring you back, Trey. You were becoming agitated."

"Are you okay, Linda, I hope I didn't scare you." Trey was worried about his wife's reaction.

"No, I'm fine, Trey. I think we should head out if we're done here, Dr. Westbrook?" Malinda said.

"Almost, Trey it seems the phone call may have started with Sonya or someone you didn't want to talk to then you were talking to someone else that you were concerned about. You didn't say the person's name you just kept calling him sir."

"I guess we can narrow that down somewhat, but I use that term a lot when I'm talking to elders, I even call my dad sir sometimes."

"Well, we've done enough for today. We can pick this up again at your next session. Don't be surprised if you start getting bits and pieces of your memory back since we've opened a path to your blockage." Dr. Westbrook said.

"Thank you, Dr. Westbrook. I'll see you on Friday." Trey and Malinda left the office then headed over to the hospital to be with their son. Trey didn't like the confused look on Malinda's face, but he decided not to get into that right now. As they headed over to the hospital, Trey wondered if it was a good thing to get his memory back.

## Chapter Twenty

Trenton and Tanya were sitting at their kitchen table the morning after Trey's first hypnosis session. With each day that passed, Trenton was confident that Trey would be acquitted. They were passing time until they headed out to the hospital to see baby Ty. Tanya took an indefinite leave from work so she could help with Malinda's care and so she could have more freedom to attend Trey's trial. She was happy that the girls were getting along better but wished she could say the same for Trey and TJ. TJ seemed to be on his brother's side, but Trey didn't trust him, so he kept TJ on the outside of his case.

No new evidence or details came through so far to help Trey's case. Trey and Trenton had an appointment with Victoria and Reuben tomorrow to finalize the witness list and to prepare Trey in case he had to testify. Victoria and Trenton were against it since Trey still hadn't gotten his memory back, but Trey insisted on telling his side of the story. Both Trenton and Tanya saw a difference in Trey since he'd been working with Dr. Westbrook and Trevor. They felt he would get his memory back soon and hopefully not have to go to trial. They stopped their conversation when they heard the doorbell. The housekeeper was out running errands so Trenton told Tanya to relax and he will get the door. He was taken totally by surprise when a distraught Sharon Young was on the other side of the door.

"Morning, Sharon. I don't think it's a good idea for you to be here." Trenton felt so sorry for Sharon. She looked like she hadn't had much sleep since this ordeal.

"Please, Trent. I just need a few minutes to talk to you and Tanya." If Trenton didn't see her with his own eyes, he wouldn't believe this was their friend talking. She sounded like she had been crying for a while and her voice was so low he could hardly hear her. Against his better judgment he moved out the way and told her she could go to the kitchen where Tanya was waiting for him to return. When Tanya saw Sharon, she stood from her chair then gave her friend a big hug.

"Have a seat, Shar." Trenton gave Tanya a look saying he didn't think they should be talking to her but decided to follow his wife's lead.

"I know it's not a good idea for me to be here, but I miss you guys. I know Trey told you that I visited him a while back. I just needed to look him in the eyes when he told me he didn't murder my daughter."

"Trey told us you dropped by. He is upset about this situation. He wanted Sonya out of his life, but he didn't want her dead." Tanya hoped she never had to feel the pain of losing one of her children. She knew it must have been much harder for Sharon since Sonya was her only child.

"I'm going to leave you ladies to talk. I'll be in the office when you're ready to go to the hospital, Tanya." Trenton was about to leave the room when Sharon asked him to stay.

"Trent, I need some advice. I hate to put you in this position, but I couldn't go to Carl because he'll take Chris's side and not listen to me."

"Shar if this is about the case, we can't talk about that." Trenton knew they were walking a thin line.

"If you can't hear me out maybe you can tell me who can. Chris has been hiding things from me. I found out yesterday that Chris knew Sonya was dying."

"Again, I need to caution you, Shar. Go talk to the police or to the prosecution if you have any evidence." Trenton said.

"I thought about that, Trent, but I don't want to get Chris into trouble."

"Shar, Trent is right. You need to go talk to the authorities." Tanya saw that her friend was in a bad way. She wished she could invite her to stay with them for a few days.

"Shar if you don't want to go to the authorities' maybe you should talk to your parents or maybe even a therapist. It seems you have a lot you need to get off your mind." Trenton wanted to help and if he was as cold blooded as some thought he was he would have let Sharon spill her guts and used the information to clear Trey's name.

"I guess I can go to my grief counselor. She's been trying to help me deal with Sonya's death, but Chris doesn't want any part of that. All he wants to do is make sure Trey goes to jail for Sonya's death. Talking to my parents won't help because they feel the same way as Chris. They knew Sonya had issues but put the blinders on instead of facing her problems." Sharon said.

"Shar, we have to go to see the baby right now, but if you're free later you can come back and have dinner with us." Tanya decided she was going to take care of her friend and not worry about the case.

"Trent is right. I shouldn't be here until the case is over. For the record, I don't think Trey murdered my baby. Thanks for hearing me out." Sharon stood then headed for the door with Tanya following behind her. When Tanya went back into the kitchen, Trenton took Tanya in his arms and softly said they were going to have to be there for Sharon because it seems like Chris was up to his neck in this mess. A few minutes later they left out to head to the hospital.

Why was it so dark in the room? Trey looked around but couldn't figure out where he was. He heard voices in the background but couldn't recognize who they belonged to. Why was his head hurting and why did he feel like he was having an out of body experience? The voices became louder, but he still couldn't make out who they belonged to. All the sudden a door slammed, and the voices seemed closer. Trey tried his best, but he couldn't figure out who was talking and why were they speaking to him in such an angry tone. He wanted to open his eyes but for some reason he couldn't. The next thing he knew someone had pushed him hard and it seemed like he was falling down a tunnel.

"Trey wake up." Malinda was shaking Trey, but he wouldn't wake up. He was sweating so badly she had to run to the linen closet to get him a towel. He was tossing and turning then he let out a loud no before he jerked himself up into a sitting position in the middle of the bed in a trance like state.

"Trey, can you hear me?" When he didn't answer Malinda sat next to him on the bed and began to gently shake him. When that didn't work, she yelled his name so loud she knew the neighbors had to hear her. She didn't care because Trey finally looked at her even though he had a distant look in his eyes.

"What happened?" Trey whispered to Malinda who had to strain to hear him.

"Trey wipe your face and I'll be right back." Malinda gave Trey the towel, grabbed her cell phone off the nightstand and went into the hall to call Trevor and Tara. She told them to come over right away because Trey needed them. She went back into the bedroom. Trey was still sitting in the same spot, but he had dried his face and upper body.

"Did I have another dream, Linda?" Trey asked.

It hurt Malinda to her soul that Trey sounded like a lost little boy. "Yes, baby you did. I called Trevor and Tara. They'll be over in a few minutes."

"Linda if you don't go stay with someone else I will. I can't be around you not knowing if I'll physically hurt you. I can take Trevor up on his offer to move in with him for a little while." Trey said.

"Baby, we can talk about that later. Go take a shower and get dressed. We can go over to the hospital when Trevor and Tara get here." Trey did as Malinda suggested. She sat on the bed with silent tears rolling down her face because she knew Trey was right. He would be better off at Trevor's. His condition seemed to worsen since the hypnosis yesterday. Hearing the doorbell, Malinda went downstairs to let her in-laws in.

## Chapter Twenty-One

Trey and Trenton were shocked when they arrived at Victoria's office. She was waiting there for them with Reuben in tow. This was the first time since the case started, they didn't have to wait on her. Trey had a disappointing night being separated from Malinda. Trevor tried his best to be entertaining, but Trey just wanted to go home. Trey was surprised he was able to sleep and didn't have any nightmares. He thought it may have to do with the relaxing atmosphere Trevor had at his condo. Trenton couldn't wait to tell the group about Sharon's visit yesterday, so he got the conversation started.

"I'm getting a bad vibe about Chris Young." Trenton went on to explain all the details of Sharon's visit.

"Wow, so we should subpoena her to be a defense witness." Reuben liked this idea.

"No, we're going to win this case without putting Sharon on the stand. She has gone through too much already." Everyone in the room was shocked by Trenton's response.

"Dad, I didn't expect you to feel this way. Ms. Sharon must have really gotten under your skin."

"Actually, she did. Shar is going to have to deal with the fact that her husband may be a part of the reason why their daughter is dead. He should have never kept the fact that Sonya was dying from his wife."

"Ok even without Mrs. Young, we still have a good case. Trey has your team come up with any new information yet?" Victoria wanted to gather as much information as possible so hopefully this won't have to go to trial. After speaking to Dr. Westbrook, Trey may not get his memory back before the trial.

"They should have that wrapped up this afternoon. I gave Tara an incentive; she could go with me to my session tomorrow if they dig up something we could use. It seems my sweet baby sister will get a kick out of seeing me not in control."

"That girl has some really strange notions. She has to be nuts to voluntarily want to go to a head shrink, no offense, son." Trenton said

"Well, as long as they come up with something, we can use who cares?" Reuben was practical about this situation.

"I hope we get farther in our session tomorrow. I've been racking my brain to figure out whom I was referring to when I said sir on that phone call."

"Things are going well so relax, Trey. I'm going to give each of you a copy of our witness list and the prosecutor's list. When you get time, go over it and see if either of you can think of any changes that need to be made. We need to finalize this list, so we can start working on their testimony. Trey we're going to save you for last since yours will be the most important and time consuming." Victoria still didn't want to put Trey on the stand if he didn't get his memory back.

"That's cool, Tori. If we're done, I want to get to the hospital. I promised to help Trevor with his class tonight." Trey was ready to get out of there. He needed to go by the office before his dad dropped him off at the hospital. He knew Trenton was going to give him a hard time about going into the office.

"Trey you need to stop worrying about not remembering what happened. I have a feeling you witnessed something that was shocking to you and it didn't help getting cracked over the head multiple times." Victoria wanted her good friend back. Everyone headed in different directions once they were finished.

Malinda stepped outside the front entrance of the hospital to get some air. She was so worried about Ty even though he was getting stronger every day. Ty now weighed four pounds and four ounces, and he was breathing much better. Malinda tried to keep negative thoughts out of her mind, but the thought of losing Ty and not being able to have another child weighed heavily on her heart. Trey reassured her that their son was going to grow to be strong, healthy, and wise. He's been so good to her and she missed him last night. This must come to an end soon, so they'll be able to focus on their son. Malinda was so deep in her thoughts she didn't hear someone coming up behind her until she was tapped on her shoulder. Turning around she was disappointed to see Malcolm.

"Lynn are you ok? I shouted your name three or four times." Malcolm said.

"What do you want, Malcolm?" Malinda hadn't seen Malcolm in a long time. He was still good looking, but he had a devilish look on his face. Although Malcolm was her first love she was attracted to Trey even when Trey didn't pay her any attention. She also hated when Malcolm called her Lynn.

"I heard you had the baby early, so I wanted to see how both of you are doing. What did you have boy or girl?" Malcolm already knew the answer, but he didn't want Malinda to know he's been keeping tabs on her.

"I'm not talking to you about my personal life, Malcolm." Malinda just wanted to get back into the hospital.

"Come on, baby. Don't be like that. I know you must need someone to talk to since your boy will be carted off to prison soon." Malcolm said with a big smile on his face.

"Move out of my way, Malcolm." Malinda tried to go around Malcolm, but he wouldn't let her get by.

"Lynn, I just want to talk..." That was all Malcolm was able to get out before CJ stepped in between them and knocked Malcolm to the ground. Before CJ could hit him again Malinda alerted security and they told Malcolm to leave. CJ escorted Malinda back upstairs to see the baby. Once they were in the family waiting room, CJ began to grill Malinda.

"Sis, why were you out there talking to that fool?" CJ asked with a mean look on his face.

"It wasn't intentional, CJ. I was getting some air when he walked up behind me saying that I can talk to him since Trey will be going to prison soon."

"Well, he looked like he was high. You need to go the other way if he tries to approach you again."

"I have no intention of saying anything to that man." Malinda jumped when Trey shouted her name as he was getting off the elevator.

"Linda are you ok? The guard downstairs told me you were involved in a scene in front of the hospital a little while ago."

"I'm good, Trey. Malcolm stopped by trying to talk to me and was getting a little hostile, but CJ took care of him." Malinda explained.

"What the hell was he doing here?" Trey didn't have time to deal with that fool.

"Trey let's talk about this later. We need to check on Ty." Malinda turned away from Trey and headed towards the ICU. Trey wanted to stay there to question CJ, but he decided to follow his wife.

Tara and Jerome were sitting in the conference room digging through the information they've found out about the background checks Trey needed for his case. Trey stopped by for a few minutes after his meeting with Victoria and Reuben but had to go to the hospital when he was alerted that Malcolm was in the area. They had been keeping a tail on all the suspects to see if they were meeting up. Jerome told Trey to make sure he stopped by after he was done at the hospital because he'd gathered some interesting information. Now as they had their piles arranged, they started with the most obvious suspect, Malcolm.

"This fool is a real nut case. He and Sonya had a lot in common. Since when do you continue to pursue a woman after she's married?" Jerome had a gut feeling that Malcolm was knee deep in this drama.

"Let's just hope his object of affection didn't give him a reason to keep pursuing her." Tara didn't think she would ever like Malinda. Now that she couldn't have any more children, she hoped she wouldn't fly off the deep end because that was the last thing her brother needed to deal with.

"Cut it out, Tara. You know how much Linda loves Trey. She wouldn't lead that fool on. Besides they had broken up before she gotten with Trey."

"I know that, but Malcolm has the means and resources to make Trey's life miserable because he wants Linda back. Maybe she hasn't closed that door completely."

"Anyway, it seems that we got something here." Jerome said to change the subject.

Tara moved closer to Jerome, so she could see what he was talking about. "Wow, whose number is that he called more than two hundred times in the last three months?"

"The phone is no longer in service. It was disconnected two days after Sonya's murder. I was able to trace the owner of the phone and it was none other than, Sonya Young." Jerome liked the sneaky smile that spread across Tara's face.

"So, now we're able to connect Malcolm to Maria and Sonya." Tara liked this news. Then they moved on to Christopher Young's pile.

"Mr. Chris has been a very busy man. I wondered if Ms. Sharon knows he took a leave of absence from work." Jerome would bet his next paycheck that Sharon didn't have any idea her husband was off from work long before Sonya's death.

"That poor lady. I feel so sorry for her." Tara said.

"He went to all of Sonya's appointments with her and has tons of calls to and from Maria's phone." Jerome was really getting into the spy stuff. Now he knows why Trey loves it so much.

"Man, what if all of these fools were in on the plot to frame Trey? They all had a motive to want Trey out of the way." Tara was getting madder by the minute.

"Let's finish looking at everything." Jerome and Tara decided to work until Trey returned.

## Chapter Twenty-Two

The room was dark and quiet. As Trey looked around, he couldn't see much. Trying to figure out his location his head began to hurt. Why did this feel like a repeat of a bad dream? He remembered leaving the office right after getting a frantic phone call from Sonya and someone else he couldn't quite remember telling him that Tara was in trouble. Any other time he wouldn't have taken a call from Sonya, but the call came through as a blocked number. Some of his clients called him this way so Trey would always answer. Sonya spoke quickly and told Trey not to hang up, she was calling about Tara. Then a male voice was on the line and said the same thing about Tara being in trouble then giving the location.

Trey remembered running out of his office and jumping into his truck to go see about his baby sister. He didn't care that the initial call came from Sonya. All he wanted to do was get to his sister. Arriving at the location of the place the caller said he would find his sister, Trey looked around and was baffled when he didn't see his sister or any sign of disturbance. Hearing loud music made Trey's head hurt even worse. Where the hell was the music coming from. The next thing Trey was conscious of was Trevor shaking him awake.

"Man, you didn't hear your loud ass alarm going off? I was knocking on your door and calling your name for the last couple of minutes." Trevor was concerned with the frighten look on Trey's face.

"What time is it, Trev?" Trey was embarrassed about his dreams. He warned Trevor before he moved in that he was taking a chance on mood swings and bad nightmares. God, he wished he was home in his own bed with his wife.

"It's almost seven o'clock so that means your alarm was going off for about half hour and you didn't hear it." Trevor didn't know how Trey was able to sleep through his alarm with that music blaring in his ear.

"I guess I didn't want to wake up until I could get more clues."

"More clues to what, Trey?" Trevor asked.

"I think my memory is coming back. I remember receiving a frantic call from Sonya. I was about to hang up when she asked me not to because she was calling because Tara was in trouble."

"Really, what else do you remember?"

"Talking to a man, but I still can't place who he was. I remember being in this dark room and my head was hurting. I tried looking around, but nothing was familiar. The next thing I remembered was being at the office that morning and receiving the call from Sonya."

"This is great, Trey. Hopefully tomorrow's session with Dr. Westbrook will help you remember everything." Trevor was happy for his baby brother.

"I sure hope so, Trev. I think I expected too much from being hypnotized so when I didn't instantly get my memory back, I saw it as a waste of time."

"Well, I'll let you get up to get your day started. Who's picking you up for the hospital?"

"Mom and Dad. They'll finally have a chance to see the baby. Mr. Corey will be there too?" Although I think Mom has been taking sneak peeps on him already Trey said smiling.

"How is Malinda's relationship coming along with her dad?"

"Pretty good. I think he's finally hearing what his children are telling him about Maria."

"Let's hope so, especially if she's involved in framing you." Trevor left Trey alone, so he could get ready while he headed out to the gym.

Trey was kind of tired by the time he and Trenton made it to his office. They had spent more than three hours at the hospital visiting with each other and the baby. Trey loved being around his family, but he was ready to get to the office to see what Tara and Jerome put together and to tell them about his dream. Trey hadn't had the time to meet with them since they went over the piles they complied of the suspects. He'd seen Tara a couple of times since Thursday, but he and Malinda were focused on the baby, so he didn't want to talk about the case. Now sitting in the conference room with his dad and Jerome, Trey was glad when Tara came into the room and closed the door behind her.

"What's this big news you have to tell us, big brother?" Tara was anxious to hear Trey's news and to tell him what she and Jerome uncovered.

"Little girl, I know you see more than your brother in this room." Trenton always had to get on his youngest daughter about her lack of manners.

"Sorry, Dad. How are you doing? Hi Rome. Now what do you have for us Trey?" Tara asked this question after she gave her dad a hug.

"Guys, I'm so happy to say that I'm starting to get my memory back."

"Boy, we've been together all morning and you didn't mention a single word about getting your memory back." Trenton didn't know what to think of his children sometimes.

"Dad, I knew I would have to go over this with these two and you were coming over with me, so I decided to tell you all together." Trey explained.

"So, what do you remember, TT?" Trey didn't like to be called TT, but he knew Jerome didn't like to be called JW so they both decided to deal with it.

"I received a call from Sonya. She knew I was about to hang up on her but before I could she said that it was about Tara and that she was in trouble. When she realized I wasn't taking her serious a man came on the phone to confirm what she told me."

"That heifer used me to lure you into her lair. Who was the man on the other end, Trey?" Tara asked.

"That I don't know, but whomever it was made the story sound authentic, so I rushed out of here and drove to the location. When I got there no one was around, and that was it because my alarm and Trev woke me up." Trey explained.

"We'll only need one guess to figure out who the male caller was? That man is up to his eyeballs in this mess. What the hell is wrong with that damn fool?" Trenton dreaded this trial and what it was going to do to Sharon when Chris involvement was exposed.

"I know, Mr. Chris doesn't like me, but I was hoping he wouldn't go this far to punish me for not loving his daughter any longer. My gut is telling me it wasn't him on the other end."

"This is all coming together now. Tara and I were able to figure out all of the people on the suspects list have been in communication with each other. I do wonder who could have been on the line if it wasn't Chris Young" Jerome was feeling good because they were finally making headway on Trey's case and his best friend had a fighting chance.

"We need to get this information to Victoria." Trenton wanted to head right over there, but knew Victoria was in court all day and there was a good chance Reuben was with her. Trey gathered the information, then jotted down a few more notes. Trenton convinced Trey to go home to rest for a while before he went back to the hospital. Tanya and Talia were there with Malinda, her dad, and brother. Carmen wanted to take off school, but Malinda told her she needed to go to school since they wouldn't let her see the baby anyway. Trey wanted to be dropped off at home instead of Trevor's. Once Trey was home he felt exhausted, so he took his dad's advice to take a nap.

At the hospital Malinda sat with Tanya and Talia in Tanya's office discussing the issues that plagued their lives. Malinda didn't want to admit it, but she was physically and emotionally drained. She didn't have her baby home with her and now Trey felt he needed to move out until he could get a handle on his emotional state. The housekeeper was there during the day and after she got out of school Carmen stayed with Malinda. CJ was there most of the time too, so Malinda didn't have a chance to get lonely, but she still missed her husband. Malinda wanted details about Ty's chances of survival. She asked both Tanya and Talia to be honest with her because all the doctors would say was, he's holding his own.

"Ms. Tanya, I need you and Talia to be completely honest with me, is Ty going to make it?" Talia's specialty was working in pediatrics, but since Tanya was head nurse over all departments, she thought she would be better able to answer the question.

"Linda the doctors are being upfront with you. Only time and God will help Ty pull through. In my many years as a nurse I've seen situations like this plenty of times, some babies made it some didn't. We must keep praying because each day that goes by Ty is getting bigger and stronger."

"I know it's just I feel so helpless. I don't know if I can go on if my baby dies. I know we could adopt, but I want my own baby with Trey."

"Linda, Ty has already beat some odds that were against him so don't give up because he's a fighter just like his mom and dad." Talia loved her nephew and prayed every day that he will grow to be strong and healthy.

Tanya was about to add to Talia's comment, but her office phone buzzed. She wondered why her assistant was bothering her since technically she was still off on leave.

"Head Nurse Taylor, the doctors need to see you and baby Taylor's mom right away." Not liking the sound of that she thanked the nurse and disconnected the call.

"Linda, we need to get to ICU. Stay calm and I'll find out what's going on." Tanya promised.

"Ok. Ms. Tanya." Linda said with tears in her eyes, she stood from the chair in front on Tanya's desk fearing her baby boy was gone.

## Chapter Twenty-Three

It was a long and stressful week for the Taylor family. Baby Ty's condition took a turn for the worst when he developed an infection which led to breathing problems. Trey could still remember the frantic call he received from Malinda on the day when Ty's condition worsened. He had only been asleep for a few hours after his dad dropped him off when the call woke him up. Even though she was upset Malinda tried her best to get Trey to stay home to wait for someone to pick him up, but he wasn't having it. He hadn't driven since Sonya's death (outside that one time he drove to the office), so Malinda didn't want him to drive when he was upset.

Trey made it to the hospital in less than fifteen minutes (usually a twenty-five-minute drive). That's when they were told Ty's infection impacted his immune system. They were doing their best to keep the infection from spreading into his bloodstream. That was on Monday now it was Friday and Ty was finally out of the woods. Trey missed a meeting with Victoria and both of his sessions with Dr. Westbrook, but he didn't care because he needed to be with his wife and son. Trey and his dad were supposed to meet with Victoria the following Monday to review any new developments and to go over the information from Tara and Jerome.

Tanya was able to talk Trey and Malinda into going home for a little while to rest and clean up because they hadn't left the hospital since Ty's emergency. The family brought them food and changes of clothes. The family was surprised to see a lot of TJ during the week. TJ knew his parents, siblings, and aunt were still mad at him, but he was sick of being the black sheep of the family, so he decided to be more supportive. Baby Taylor was still in NICU, but his infection was cleared, and he was breathing better while steadily gaining weight. Trey and Malinda hoped that once Ty reached four pounds ten ounces, he would be able to come home. The doctors said as long as he was breathing steadily, he would be able to go home even if he wasn't the standard five pounds. They were going to hire a baby nurse to the disappointment of Tanya and Talia. They wanted to be the ones to take care of the baby, but Trey and Malinda wanted their families to return to their normal lives, especially since the trial would be starting soon.

After making it home, Trey and Malinda went into their bedroom to get used to being back in there together. He told Malinda he was coming back home once Ty was out of the woods. Sleeping in his own bed on Monday after his dad dropped him off made Trey realize it was time for him to come home. He hoped the dreams wouldn't be so disruptive since he was slowly regaining his memory. Now sitting on the loveseat in their sitting room that was attached to their master bedroom, Trey decided to ask Malinda how she felt about his decision to come home.

"Trey, I'm glad you decided it was time for you to come home. I didn't want you to leave in the first place. Your situation is just a bump in the road that we both should deal with together as a family."

"I know baby, but I was afraid of what my dreams would lead to. Trevor said sometimes I scared the shit out of him when I woke up screaming my head off."

"Well, I'm glad that Dr. Westbrook could switch your Tuesday appointment to Monday, before you and your dad meet with Victoria."

"I don't know about this hypnosis thing. It seems like since I've been getting that treatment my dreams are more intense. Sometimes I'm scared to close my eyes."

"Dr. Westbrook told you this may happen. Either you will get your memory back in bits and pieces or it all may come rushing back at the same time. Of course, it's safer for you if you get your memories back piece by piece even though it's more frustrating."

"Well, I don't know about you, but all I want to do is to take a quick shower and sleep the rest of the day away. Are you game?" With a smile on her face Malinda grabbed Trey's hand then pushed him towards the bathroom.

The trio met in a dark and deserted area. They didn't want to be seen together taking the risk of being exposed. Over the last few weeks they've been blaming each other for the way their plan was falling apart. Now all of them were terrified they would be caught. So many unexpected things had occurred where they had no control. Being an egomaniac, the leader of the bunch decided it was time to speak of the displeasure of the perfectly developed plan crumbling into little pieces.

"What the hell is wrong with you fools? Why can't you all follow the simplest of instructions?"

"Yelling at us isn't going to make the situation better." The first person didn't want to hear this shit right now because life has been hell over the last three months.

"I don't want to hear that bullshit. You've been the weakest link from the beginning." The leader had no problem with assigning blame.

"The hell I have. I'm not the one who's screwing everything up by knocking the sense out of that bastard."

"You guys need to cut it out. We're still in the driver's seat. If they had all the facts, they would've been able to file a motion of dismissal." This came from the third person who was quiet while the other two acted a fool.

"Oh, now you want to sound confident. You weren't talking like that a week ago when you blew up my damn phone whining about this one over here." The leader was just as tired of fool number two as he was with fool number one.

"Oh, now we want to continue to point fingers at each other. None of this will work out to our advantage if we start to get sloppy." The third voice was frustrated with his crazy ass partners-in-crime.

"What do you mean start. We've been sloppy for a while now since you idiots haven't followed the plan."

"While you're placing the blame on us what about you? You said all of this would be a piece of cake, but it's been one problem after the other. We need to do something right now before all goes to hell if that bastard gets his memory back."

"You better watch yourself. We're still on track since the trial will start in less than two weeks. They haven't been able to focus on the case as much lately with all the problems with the baby." The leader felt bad for the baby, but that baby's dad must pay for toying with other people lives.

"Let's meet back here in a couple of days. I'll remind you two to be discreet from here on out." The trio left going in separate directions, hoping their plan doesn't fall apart.

The four siblings sat at the table in the local diner after finishing their meal. TJ asked them to meet up so they could talk about the issues within the family. He figured they all needed to pull together especially since the situation with Ty was touch and go. He expected to get grief from Tara and maybe even Trevor, but he knew he deserved it because not only his actions during the case, but also because of the way he's always treated Trey. He jumped right into what he wanted to speak to them about.

"Guys, I know that you all are wondering why I asked you to come here today." TJ said.

"I bet it's because you want us to plead your case to Trey." Tara knew her brother well, so she got right to the point.

"Why do you have to say that with such an attitude baby girl?" TJ thought he was ready to deal with his baby sister's attitude, but she was getting on his nerve already.

"You should've supported our brother from the beginning. That's why your hardheaded behind is here now seeking our help." This time Tara threw an evil stare at Talia.

"Little girl you need to watch who you are cutting your eyes at. Mom and Dad aren't here to save you."

"I can do what I want to with my eyes. For the record I don't need anyone saving me from you."

"That's enough. The two of you go into your separate corners and give TJ a chance to say what he has to say, so we can get out of here." Trevor was just as disappointment in TJ and Talia as Tara, but not as outspoken.

"As I was saying, I can be of help with Trey's case if he lets me. All I need you guys to do is talk him into letting me help so we all can clear his name." TJ had his pride. He wasn't willing to go any further to seek his siblings help.

"Let me place my vote now. I can't in good faith talk Trey into something that he feels is wrong, so I won't be pressuring him with all the drama he has going on in his life." Tara sat with her arms folded in front of her with a frown on her face.

"I'll talk to him, TJ. I don't know how much good it will do because he's adamant that he doesn't want anyone working on his case that doesn't believe whole heartily in his innocence." Talia was almost in TJ's position. If it wasn't for Malinda, she would have been left out in the cold too.

"I'll bring it up to him, man, but I won't pressure him if he still feels strongly against your getting involved." Trevor was ready to go so he hoped they were almost finished with this unexpected meeting.

"Thanks, everyone. You guys can leave, and I'll take care of the check." TJ expected a little more, but what he got was better than what he had when they started. He didn't expect anything from Tara and that's what he got. As they headed out in their separate directions, they hoped that this will be over soon, so their brother could focus on his wife and son.

## Chapter Twenty-Four

It was a week before the trial was scheduled to begin. Trey hadn't worked with Victoria or Reuben since Ty's relapse. He knew his dad would keep on top of everything and since he hadn't gotten his memory back the trial was inevitable. He and Malinda spent most of the weekend with Ty. They couldn't believe how strong he was getting after being so ill only a few days ago. The way he was growing he would be home in no time. This week Trey would focus on his defense. Malinda told him she and the rest of her family would keep an eye on the baby while he does whatever was needed to clear his name. Trey still refused TJ's help even after Trevor and Talia told him about their meeting. Trey didn't have time to deal with his brother acting like an immature fool. He was fighting for his life and the welfare of his wife and son.

Sitting in the conference room at his firm waiting on Jerome and Tara to show up, Trey thought about all he had to lose. He wished he could remember what happened that day. Whenever he tried too hard to remember that's when he began to get those horrible headaches. He was frustrated because since the dream about Tara he hadn't had any other memories. Dr. Westbrook said tomorrow's session would be the last time she will put him under. She explained that when he was getting close to remembering what happened that day, his behavior was so unsettling she didn't want him to force anything because that could do more harm than good. Trey was so deep into his thoughts he didn't hear Beverly knocking at the door until she tapped him on his shoulder.

"What's the matter with you, Trey? Didn't you hear me knocking and calling your name?" Beverly didn't like the spaced out look on her boss's face.

"Sorry, Bev. I was trying to think about what happened that day, so I won't have to go to trial next week."

"That's ok, boss. I was just a little concerned when I kept knocking with no answer and I knew you were in here." Beverly explained.

"We're coming down to the wire and we have some leads, but not enough to stop the trial. I just pray that Mr. Chris isn't involved in this mess because that's the last thing Ms. Sharon needs to deal with."

"I wouldn't put it pass him. I don't know what made him change, but he's not the same person he was years ago."

"I feel Sonya was telling him a lot of things that wasn't true about our relationship. I used to be so close to both of her parents, but when I became engaged to Linda that seemed to change overnight even though Sonya and I hadn't been together for years."

"It makes you wonder if her illness had anything to do with her stalking you and Linda. I mean that chick was on some special kind of stuff with all the outrageous things she was doing."

"I guess we'll never find that out now. Tori still wanted to call Ms. Sharon as a witness, but I think we would be better off calling Mr. Chris as a hostile witness. He's so volatile I think she will be able to trip him up."

"I know I shouldn't say anything, but your baby sister has a surprise for you this morning. She thinks she has recreated the entire scene before and after the crime and that's why she wanted you here so early to go over everything."

"That girl. I don't know what I would do without all of you having my back."

"We have to have your back. You're our bread and butter." After that statement Beverly told Trey she had to get back to her desk, so she could earn her paycheck. Trey looked at his watch and wondered what was keeping his sister and best friend.

Trey was sitting at a diner near Victoria's office killing time until they met later that afternoon. His dad wasn't going to be able to make it since he had a doctor's appointment his mom refused to let him cancel. Trey's head was still spinning from the demonstration given by Tara and Jerome earlier. He felt some of what they came up with was possible because every time he remembered something from that day he would get terrible headaches. He wondered if things would work out before he had to go to trial next week. He couldn't see that happening if he didn't get his memory back. Last week was the first time he's been on his own as far as driving himself around. Just as Trey was finishing up his coffee and about to go to pay his bill, the last person he wanted to see stepped in front of him.

"I need a few minutes with you, Trey." Maria had to give this a try because Malinda still wasn't speaking to her and she missed her favorite niece.

"We have nothing to talk about, Maria." Trey sounded bored and that pissed Maria off.

"I want to see my niece, and her baby, Trey." Maria persisted.

"Well you're talking to the wrong person. You know why Linda stopped talking to you. I'm not going to pressure her to do so when we're going through so much right now."

"All the more reason she needs me, Trey." Maria insisted.

"No, she has her brother, sister, dad, and my family. That's all the support she needs."

"You're the reason why she's not talking to me you selfish bastard." Maria yelled.

"No, you're the reason why she kicked you to the curb. How do you think it made all of them feel you pouncing on their dad as soon as they lost their mom? Very tacky, Maria."

"You don't know what the hell you're talking about. Getting involved with you was the worst decision Mindy ever made. She was happy with Malcolm until you came along and destroyed that."

"I'm not going to argue with you, Maria. Just leave us alone." With that Trey left to go to pay his check. He didn't turn back to see the hateful look Maria was giving him.

Trey was feeling the beginning of another headache after talking to Maria. He wondered when she was going accept that her relationship changed with Malinda when she targeted her dad before her mom's body was cold in the ground. The hate he saw in her face made him realize she could be in on the plot to get rid of him. The woman was psycho because Malinda and Malcolm weren't seeing each other when she and Trey first started dating. From what Malinda had told him, they hadn't been together for almost a year. Either way, what in the world was Maria so obsessed about because Malinda didn't have a relationship with Malcolm before he came into the picture?

Trey was waiting in the lobby of Victoria's office for her to return. He took this opportunity to think about all the suspects in his case. Of course, Malcolm was at the top of his list. What this fool failed to realize even if he was convicted and sent to prison, Malinda still wouldn't take him back. Even from a prison cell Trey would make sure he wouldn't be anywhere near his son. Trey needed to think about something else because this subject was making his head hurt worse. He tried doing some of the breathing exercises Trevor showed him but that didn't make his head feel any better.

Trey rested back on the nice soft chair and wished for his headache to go away. He must have dosed off because the next thing he knew Victoria's assistant was shaking him awake saying that he was shouting for someone not to do it. He was too embarrassed to ask what else he was shouting about so he asked if he could wait in Victoria's office. The assistant said that was fine because Victoria called to say she would be there in five minutes. Trey was alone for only a few minutes when Victoria came into her office with an armful of folders.

"What's this I hear about you screaming your head off a few minutes ago?" Victoria had a smile in her voice when she asked Trey that question.

"Tori this isn't funny. I think more of my memory is trying to come back because every time I get a bad headache, I seem to remember more about what happened that day."

"That's good, Trey. With a week before your trial we need all the help we can get. If you can remember what happened, it would be a blessing."

"Tell me about it. I had a run in with Linda's, Aunt Maria. I have a feeling she is knee deep in this mess just like Malcolm and Mr. Chris."

"You may be right, but it's all about proving it. I think it would be a good idea to call all the suspects to the stand."

"I think you're right about that because with so much hate in all of them you shouldn't have too much trouble tripping them up except maybe Malcolm. He's slick and knows his way around the law."

"He won't be as tough as you think because he's arrogant and thinks that the world owes him because he's the son of a powerful judge. I want to keep our witness list short because the prosecution's case is falling apart, and I think they know it too because he wants to meet with me Wednesday and I'm sure it's about pleading down." Victoria said.

"Let me make this perfectly clear, Tori. I don't care what the offer is I'm not pleading guilty. I will not do that to myself or my family."

"I understand that, Trey, but you know this is all part of the process."

"I need to go to the hospital to relieve Linda. Email me and my dad the final witness list and any other information you want me to review. I'll look over everything and we can discuss it on Thursday when dad and I get finished with Dr. Westbrook. I still can't believe he wants to go to my last session."

"Maybe because it is your last session. You know he wanted to be involved with everything regarding the case."

"Ok, Tori thanks for everything. I'll be in touch." Victoria came from behind her desk and gave Trey a hug and told him to be sure to let her know when they will allow visitors outside of the family to see Ty. After agreeing to keep Victoria updated Trey left her office and headed to the hospital.

## Chapter Twenty-Five

It was finally Thursday and the last day of Trey's therapy session. He was excited and sad at the same time because he'd gotten used to coming in to see Dr. Westbrook twice a week. A lot has happened since his first day with her and all week. Trey was still getting little bits and pieces of his memory back. It wasn't enough for him, but he knew there was nothing he could do about it. Trevor wanted to come to this session too, but Dr. Westbrook didn't want Trey's concentration to be deterred. Ty was getting bigger and stronger as each day passed. The doctors said if he continued to gain weight and breathe on his own, he may be able to go home in a few weeks. This was the best news the family could hear.

While Trey and Trenton were at this session Malinda and CJ had a meeting with their dad. He told them there were things going on they didn't understand so it was time for a family talk. Malinda and CJ agreed, but they all decided Carmen shouldn't be there. They made it clear that Maria couldn't be there. Malinda was pissed when Trey told her about his run in with Maria. She just wanted that lady to stay out of their lives. Trey was at peace most of the times until he started having his headaches. He had a feeling this was it and soon he would remember everything. When he did it may be bad news for a lot of people they knew. The men stopped talking when Dr. Westbrook walked into her office. Trey introduced his dad who changed in his disposition once she entered. Trey had to smile because his dad for all his strengths was uncomfortable around doctors even though his wife and oldest daughter were in the medical profession.

"Trey how have things being going in your life since your last visit?" Dr. Westbrook wanted to start off nice and easy because there was nothing more she could do for Trey since hypnosis wasn't successful.

"Getting back bits and pieces of my memory. The more I remember the more frightening it gets."

"How are you feeling about the upcoming trial?"

"Well, I was so hoping that we would solve the case before we had to go to trial but that doesn't seem likely."

"I don't think I have to tell you that once you do remember the pain both physical and mental won't just disappear. Your mind is blocking out something that was terrifying to you, so I just hope you're in a safe and welcoming environment when the bulk of your memories returns."

"Dr. Westbrook, what are the chances my son's memory blockage has to do with the injury he suffered instead of the events that took place that day?" Trenton felt he already knew the answer to that question but wanted a professional opinion.

"In my opinion the blows to the head aren't the reason why Trey doesn't have his memory back. I think whatever he was witness to was too much for him, and instead of dealing with the issue he is protecting himself from it." Dr. Westbrook explained.

"That's Tori's opinion too. Since the few memories I have has to do with an older person she feels that Sonya's dad is that person I'm protecting by not remembering."

"Well, I certainly hope not. That fool is running loose making all kinds of trouble. I told Tanya to prepare Sharon for his downfall because I'll bet a month's pay that he's probably the ringleader in this conspiracy." Trenton couldn't stand the man Chris had become.

"I sure hope that's not the case. Mr. Chris used to be such a nice man before Sonya started to lose her way. Ms. Sharon would be all alone if he's found guilty and sent away." Trey knew his family would rally around her, but it wouldn't be the same.

"You shouldn't be worried about that, son. Your mom and I will make sure Sharon will be okay." Trenton would like to talk more about what Trey could do to get the rest of his memory back.

Dr. Westbrook put Trey under again but as with the previous attempt she had to bring him out because he became agitated.

"Trey, I've put together some exercises that will help you when you get painful headaches. Make sure you keep up your program with your brother. If you feel you need to come back to see me just make an appointment."

"I may take you up on that. The closer the trial date nears the more anxious I get."

"That's normal. Just remember to take it in stride and use the powerful support system you have backing you up. There's always the fear of the unknown in situations like yours, but if you stay focused, you'll be fine." Trey and Trenton made their way to the door and thanked Dr. Westbrook for her help.

While Trey and Trenton were at his therapy session Malinda, CJ, and Corey Sr., met at Trey's and Malinda's. They decided not to have Carmen at the meeting since they would be talking about adult issues. Plus, they didn't want to take Carmen out of school. Carmen would have preferred to be with the rest of the family, but Malinda insisted on her not being there so the adults would be able to talk openly. They were seated at the dining room table. Malinda starting off the conversation.

"Dad what do you want to meet with us about?"

"I know you guys have been upset with me about my relationship with Maria." Corey Sr. responded.

"That's an understatement. The more you try to force that woman on us the more you're pushing all of us away. You should be focused on Carmen and Linda not that woman." CJ didn't care if his words and tone upset his dad.

"CJ let's tone it down a bit and hear what dad has to say." Malinda was going to have to work hard to keep things under control since her dad and brother had bad tempers.

"Son are you here to listen or to place blame at my feet?" Corey Sr. asked.

136

"The blame is on you, so you don't have to worry about me placing it anywhere else. Carmen is at a difficult age right now. She's going to need all of us to be on our game to get her through her teenage years. Times aren't like they use to be when Linda and I were growing up."

"Son, I'm not trying to be ignorant to your sister's needs. I'm trying to do the best I can. Your mom wouldn't have wanted me to live like a recluse."

"Wait a minute, Dad. I don't think this is a good time to bring up mom. You can't tell me that she wouldn't be upset if you were messing around with her baby sister? We're not upset because you've moved on, but with the person you moved on with." Malinda didn't like the route this conversation was taking.

"That's where you're wrong, Linda. Your mom knew about me and your aunt." The shocked looks on Linda and CJ's faces would have been funny if the situation wasn't so serious.

"How did mom find out about that sick shit?" CJ was fit to be tied.

A sad look crossed their dad's face before he answered CJ's question, "She walked in on us the day Carmen was born."

"No, Dad. Please tell me you weren't cheating on mom with her." Malinda refused to say her aunt's name.

"I made a terrible mistake, kids. I was truly sorry for my actions."

"The hell you were. You're still running around with that scant and you have the nerve to want our understanding. I can't speak for Linda or Carmen, but your actions are so horrendous I have nothing else to say to you. Linda please let Carmen stay here with you and Trey. Once I get settled somewhere else, I can take her if you want me to." CJ said.

"Son, I understand your being upset, but you or your sister will not be removing my daughter for her home."

"Linda, I'll talk to you later." Without replying to his dad's comments CJ left Malinda and their dad alone.

"Linda you have to know I didn't want to hurt your mom, but we had grown apart. When we decided to end things, she found out she was pregnant with your sister. You guys may thing Maria is the wrong choice for me to make, but what you need to understand is that I was dating Maria before I married your mom." Corey Sr. was looking for sympathy, but from the look on Malinda's face he wasn't going to get it.

"Dad none of that matters. If I understand you correctly, you and that woman are responsible for my mom's death?"

"No, Linda that's not true. Your mom died when her placenta ruptured. They couldn't control the bleeding after Carmen was born."

"Dad, please do me a big favor and let Carmen move in with me and Trey for a little while. I could use the help when the baby comes home." Malinda decided to go at her dad in a different direction.

"Linda, I know what you're trying to do, but I don't want to be separated from my baby."

"Think about what's best for Carmen. We can see you aren't going to stop seeing that woman and it's disrespectful to keep bringing her around."

"That was a chance meeting last time. I didn't expect anyone to be at my house."

"Dad, please think about what I said. I have to get back to the hospital because the doctor wants to go over some things with me and Trey."

"I'll think about it. I'll see how Carmen feels. I love all of you guys Linda, but you need to respect the decisions I make about my personal life." Corey gave Malinda a brief hug before he headed home to talk to his daughter once she got home from school.

## Chapter Twenty-Six

Trey woke up early on the day of his trial. Mondays have never been his best day and today was worse than most. The weekend went by fast, but the best part of it was that Ty was doing much better. He gained weight and his breathing had improved. The worst part of the weekend was consoling Malinda after she talked with her dad. He still hadn't agreed to let Carmen move in with them, but Malinda was still holding out hope he would change his mind. CJ took the talk even worse than Malinda. He moved out of his dad's house and was now living in a hotel room while apartment hunting. Malinda tried to get him to move in with her and Trey, but he declined.

Going over his case, Trey was a little upset that it had gotten this far. When he entered his not guilty plea at his preliminary hearing and told Victoria under no circumstances would he accept a plea bargain, the process continued forward to a trial. The prosecution refused to offer a plea bargain anyway because they felt they had an open and shut case. All the pre-trial motions Victoria filed failed to Trey's disappointment. They were looking at a much better case than when Trey was first charged, but they still had their work cut out for them.

Malinda went to the hospital to see Ty early and was going to meet Trey at the courthouse. Trey tried his best to get her to stay with the baby, but she said her place was by his side, plus Talia was on duty so, she would keep an eye on Ty. Trey decided he couldn't put off getting ready any longer because his parents would be there to pick him up soon. The family decided to ride over together so Trevor and Tara will be with them. He didn't know if TJ would show up or not and since Talia had to work, she wouldn't be there. Jerome was working on some last-minute details, so he would meet them at the courthouse. Trey was just walking down the stairs when he heard his dad blowing the horn. After looking around and grabbing his keys he left the house. Before he could get comfortable Tara started.

"Good morning, Trey. Remember what we talked about. Just stay calm and look each juror in their eyes with a confident look on your face at all times."

"Chill, baby sister. You know between dad, Victoria, and Reuben our brother is well prepared for today." Trevor loved his baby sister, but sometimes she didn't know when to keep her mouth closed. The family made small talk until they arrived at the courthouse, parked, and made their way through tons of reporters trying to get a statement. Victoria and Reuben met them at the door then took them into a small waiting room until it was time for them to go into the courtroom.

"Let's start with what's going to happen today. We are looking to select twelve jurors and at least two alternates. These jurors will be asked by the judge if serving on the jury would present a hardship on them. Then they will be asked questions to determine if their attitudes or experiences might lead them to be biased in this case." Victoria had already explained all of this to Trey even though she didn't have to since he's been in law enforcement, but it's different when you're on trial instead of a perp.

"So, you think we'll be able to select a panel of jurors today?" Trey asked this question because he knew sometimes it was difficult to select a panel of jurors both sides would agree to.

"Yes, I do. After the judge ensures the jury panel is legally qualified to serve, the panel will be turned over to the defense and prosecution to question." Victoria could see that Tara, Trevor, and Tanya were nervous. Since Trey and Trenton were more adapted to the process, they were taking all of this in stride.

"I've read that this can be a tedious process and sometimes it's difficult to get both sides into agreement." Trevor had been reading a lot lately about criminal law, so he could get a better understanding of the system.

"That's correct. What's even more of a challenge now is the number of preemptory challenges were reduced from ten to seven. Preemptory challenges allow each side to dismiss jurors who may be qualified but appear too likely to favor the opposing party." Reuben broke this explanation down so everyone in the room could understand.

"We also have to look out for jurors that have actual and implied bias. Jurors with actual bias admit that they wouldn't be able to be impartial. Jurors with implied bias have character traits or personal experiences that make it unlikely for them to be able to be impartial, regardless of what they say during the vior dire, (jury selection process). Victoria was glad they had a few minutes to talk because Trey seemed a little calmer." Before anything else could be said, a court guard came into the room to tell Victoria it was time for them to go in.

The group met again, but this time all five of them were there. This was a very important day for most of them because they prayed it was the beginning of the end for Trey Adrian Taylor. Only one person in attendance wasn't happy to be there, but the others didn't care because this individual played an important part in putting their plan together. The leader stood up happy and proud like he was about to speak to a roomful of people, "We're down to the nitty gritty. For a minute there I thought they were going to let that fool go."

"There wasn't a chance of that because he's still walking around like an idiot not remembering anything about that day." Another voice spoke up. This person liked to be called The Eliminator.

"Are you sure about that? The defense could just be waiting to spring something on us at the trial." This time the voice came from the one person that didn't want to be there.

"Hell, yeah I'm sure. I have it on good authority. I have someone that's close to the family keeping an eye out on things."

"You said the same thing about the mistakes that were made. You were sure about it those times too." The person that didn't want to be there, wanted to make all of them as uncomfortable as possible.

"I've had about enough of your ungrateful ass. You better remember you're just as involved in all of this as the rest of us." The leader said.

"Not by choice. I don't think it's a good idea for us to go to the trial especially not together." The person continued.

"No one cares about what you to think." This came from the leader.

"It's time to get this show on the road. Let's split up like we agreed then watch the high and mighty fall." This came from the one person in the room that felt he had the most to gain from watching Trey fall and fall hard. Once he was finished with Trey, he had another person on his list to get even with. He didn't care that that person was related to the most important person in his life.

Trey sat at the defense table with Victoria and Reuben while on the other side of the room Glenn Gordon sat alone at the prosecution table. Trey was surprised that Sonya's parents wasn't there yet. TJ had joined the family as well as some of Trey's high school friends and a few of his clients. Beverly stayed at the office to keep things moving there but, told Tara and Jerome when the trial started, they were going to have to alternate because she wasn't going to miss the entire thing. They expected Judge Walter Blackwell to preside over the case and to arrive in the courtroom shortly. Trey felt confident since Malinda was there sitting in the first row directly behind him with his parents, Trevor, Tara, and Jerome. TJ sat on the second row with Trey's other supporters because he arrived late. They were all ordered to stand when the judge appeared in the courtroom. After everyone was seated the judge asked that the panel of prospective jurors to be brought into the courtroom.

The judge started off by thanking the prospective jurors for their service then began to ask questions ensuring they were legally qualified to serve. He followed by asking if their serving on the jury would cause them undue hardship. After the judge was done with his questioning, he turned the floor over to the prosecution and defense. Judge Blackwell was known for being hardnosed but fair. Victoria examined the prospective jurors and felt confident they would be able to select an impartial jury.

The prosecution and defense began questioning each prospective juror about their biases and backgrounds as well as what they knew about the case. They asked questions to uncover characteristics or experiences that might cause potential jurors to favor the prosecution or the defense. It took most of the morning, but so far, they only selected four out of the twelve jurors and two alternates needed. They recessed for lunch and were scheduled to resume at one o'clock.

## Chapter Twenty-Seven

Trey wondered why his head was hurting so badly. There was darkness all around him. He could hear people talking in the background but couldn't understand what they were saying. Where the hell was, he was all he could think about. The last thing he remembered was coming over to the address he was given by the male caller. Trey tried to place his voice which sounded familiar but couldn't. There was loud music coming from the address he was given. He didn't see anyone around but wondered if the neighbors would call the police about the loud music. He remembered when he was on the force, he had to answer frivolous complaints of loud music. As he approached the house the door was cracked, he knocked and called Tara's name but didn't get an answer then he called out Sonya's name and still didn't get an answer. He lightly pushed the door open and carefully walked in with his gun drawn. He remembered being pushed from behind and everything went blank.

Malinda was abruptly awakened by Trey's tossing and turning. She called his name and when he still seemed to be caught up in his dream, she started to shake him. Trey yelled no to the top of his lungs and the next thing he knew he was looking into his wife's startled face. He hated that look because he knew it was another dream and his wife appeared to be afraid of him.

"What happened, Linda?" Trey's head was hurting, and he felt like he was getting over a drunken hangover.

"You had another bad dream, baby. Do you feel like talking about it?" Malinda sat up in bed next to Trey, so she could get comfortable and he did the same.

"This time I remembered a little bit more about what happened that day. I remembered hearing loud music coming from the address I was given. As I approached the front door, I saw that it was cracked. I pulled out my revolver and slowly walked into the house. I was pushed from behind then everything went black." Trey was shaken by the memory.

"Wow, baby before you know it you're going to remember everything that happened that day. Then we can put a halt to this trial, so we can concentrate on our son." Malinda wished that day was today.

"There was something so familiar about that male voice, but I still can't place it."

"It'll come to you, baby. I'm going to head to the shower so I can go see Ty before coming to court. I'm a little nervous leaving him since your mom or sister won't be on duty."

"Honey it's early on and most of the family will be there. Why don't you stay at the hospital with the baby? I'll have the family keep you posted? I don't like our son being left alone neither."

"Are you sure, Trey? I don't want you to feel like I'm abandoning you."

"I'm sure. Now that the jury has been selected our illustrious DA will put on an elaborate show when making his opening statement, but I know Tori can handle anything he can dish out."

"Ok, baby. Make sure the family keeps me posted." Malinda jumped out of bed after giving Trey a kiss then headed for the shower.

When Trey arrived at the courthouse, he was glad to see that his family was already there. He drove himself today so he could go to the office and hospital later. After speaking to them for a few minutes Victoria asked him and Trenton to meet with her for a few minutes before court got underway. Following her into the same small waiting room next to the courtroom they used yesterday, Victoria had a smile on her face when she told Trey that he looked well rested. He told her maybe it was because he remembered a few more tidbits and that Malinda would be staying with the baby, so he didn't have to worry about that. Getting down to the reason she wanted to see them since she knew they only had a few minutes, Victoria opened her brief case and took some papers out.

"I feel good about the panel we selected yesterday."

"Yes, getting that many women on the jury should work in Trey's favor." Trenton said with a big smile on his face.

"Yes, and not only that, I think the DA made a big mistake with his male selections. It seemed as though he was just striving to get as many men on the panel instead of making sure that he had the most qualified people to hear the case." Now it was Victoria's turn to have a big smile on her face.

"We're lucky to have a diverse group. I think this will work in our favor. With seven women and five men it should be an interesting deliberation if the case gets that far." Trenton was hoping that something big would happen to have the case thrown out like Trey getting his full memory back or the fools that set him up makes a major mistake.

"Let's not get overconfident because people are fickle and sometimes it's hard to figure out what's going on in their heads." Trey wanted to be cautious because one mistake could cause him his freedom.

"You're right my friend. I'm not going to let my guard down or let anything happen to my best PI." Victoria wanted Trey to relax a little before he went into the courtroom, which was now since the guard came in to tell them they were ready to get started. Gathering her papers, the trio left the small room hoping luck would be on their side.

The judge appeared in the courtroom followed by the jury. Both sides said they were ready to get started with their opening statements. The prosecutor was scheduled to present their case against Trey first. He had a satisfying look on his face like there was no way in the world he would lose this case with all the evidence he had. Sometimes Trey felt the same way, but he would never let that show on his face. He sat tall in his seat between Victoria and Reuben. Looking over at the jury as the DA began, Trey listened closely to the opening statement.

"Mr. Trey Adrian Taylor is a murderer. The evidence in this case will show that there are people in this world that think they know him best but know him in the least. You're going to hear testimony that Mr. Taylor on the morning of Monday, August twenty-fourth, with willful intent took the life of Ms. Sonya Elaine Young by shooting her to death. Mr. Taylor was found at the scene of the crime with the murder weapon his hand lying next to the deceased body of Ms. Young. His fingerprints were the only prints on the murder weapon. When the police arrived on the scene, Mr. Taylor was unconscious. The State will prove that no one other than Mr. Taylor committed this crime. He had motive, means, and opportunity. He has no witnesses to prove his whereabouts from the time he left his office until he regains consciousness in the hospital. The police will tell you about the evidence found at the crime scene including the murder weapon."

"Mr. Taylor expects this court to believe that he has no memory of the day of the crime. You ask why a man with Mr. Taylor's standing commit such a horrendous crime? It's simple, to keep his ongoing affair quiet with the deceased. We will prove that Mr. Taylor's claims of not wanting anything to do with the deceased is untrue and that on the day of the murder, Mr. Taylor was in fact having a romantic interlude with the deceased. The State will show that there is more than enough physical evidence to prove Mr. Taylor committed this crime. As previously stated, his fingerprints were the only prints on the murder weapon and there's no evidence that anyone else was present during the time of the crime. Although Mr. Taylor claims to have no memory of the crime, known to be an upstanding member of the community, and a successful businessman it didn't help Sonya Young who lost her life. Why did Ms. Young have to die? Is it because Mr. Taylor was so afraid of their secret affair exploding in his face?"

Looking at the jury's faces, Trey could see how some of the DA's statements moved them. He knew Tori would have a powerful comeback and she would need it. This is the first chance Trey looked around to see who was sitting on the prosecution side. Of course, right in the front seat were Sonya's parents. There were a few people that they went to school with and some others he didn't know. Glancing towards the back of that side of the room, Trey wasn't surprised to see Malcolm, but he was shocked to see Maria sitting right beside him glaring his way. They looked so out of place sitting together, but Trey didn't have the time or the patience to think about that because Tori was about to make her opening statement.

"Good morning, my name is Victoria Hamilton. I'm here to represent Mr. Trey Adrian Taylor who is being falsely accused of murder. At the end of this case, we are confident that we will be able to ask for a verdict of not guilty. Ladies and gentlemen of the jury, this case is about the death of Sonya Elaine Young. The prosecution hopes to present an open and shut case against Mr. Taylor, but that will not be the case. They will tell you to ignore the fact that Mr. Taylor suffered an injury that left him with memory loss. The defense will call Dr. Larissa Westbrook to the stand that will support the fact that my client suffers from memory loss due to the injury he received on the day of the crime. My client is a law-abiding citizen that served three years on the Chicago Police force and now owns a private investigation firm that is doing quite well. He's a husband and a father of a newborn son. He comes from a respected family with ties to the community."

"We're not denying that my client and Ms. Young had an unusual relationship, but we will show that Mr. Taylor did everything within his power to deter the obsessive behaviors of the deceased. Mr. Gordon would have you believe there is no other possible suspect in this case, but that's simply not true. It's true that my client was found unconscious next to the deceased by the police just as the prosecution has stated, but testimony will show that he was cleverly framed for this crime. At the end of this case we would ask that you find Mr. Taylor innocent. The state will not be able to meet its burden of proof, and we would ask for a verdict of not guilty. Thank you."

## Chapter Twenty-Eight

Court was in recess for the morning and scheduled to resume at one o'clock. Since they had almost two hours to kill, Chris and Sharon decided to go home to eat instead of going out. The fifteen-minute ride home was silent. They had been arguing about the case for the last few weeks. Chris was beside himself because his wife had the nerve to have doubts about that fool's guilt. Here it was their baby girl was brutally murdered, and his wife was giving him lip about the wrong person being on trial and not wanting to attend. As soon as they walked into the house Chris got started.

"Shar, I don't want to hear any nonsense about you not going back to court. We have to be there together to be a voice for our daughter since she isn't here to speak for herself."

"I'm not going to let you bully me into your way of thinking. I don't know what's been going on with you lately, but you seemed to forget I'm your wife not your child."

"I don't want to hear this bullshit right now. The prosecution has that bastard dead to rights, so you're going to have to accept that he committed this crime and will be held accountable."

"Chris, we've known the Taylors for a long time as well as their children. Trey isn't capable of committing a crime like this and you know it."

"I don't know anything of the sort. They wouldn't have him on trial if they didn't have enough evidence to prove he's guilty. What more do you want, woman. He was the only one at the crime scene with the murder weapon in his hand when the police arrived."

"That doesn't mean he was the only one there when our baby was murdered. Trey has never portrayed any violent tenancies even when Sonya was taking him through the ringer."

"I can't believe my ears. You're buying into the hype that he's innocent. Woman you have to get it together and stay away from those people because they're filling your mind with nonsense."

"I'm not naive or gullible so don't act like I don't have a mind of my own. I've had doubts from the beginning and after talking to Trey, I don't think he's guilty." Sharon insisted.

Chris stood and started pacing around the room. This was getting to be too much for him to deal with. "I can't talk to you right now. Maybe it's best you don't come back to the trial because I know our angel is looking down on you and is very disappointed that you're not trying to avenge her death." Chris walked out the front door leaving his wife with tears rolling down her face.

The family went out for a bite to eat while they were waiting for court to reconvene. They parked the two cars (Trenton and Trey's) in the courthouse parking garage and headed for the elevators. Trey was walking slowly behind his family because he felt another headache coming on. He was walking behind Tara and Jerome as they all stopped at the elevator. There were other people standing waiting with them so when one of the elevator doors opened, he told his parents, Talia, Trevor, and Tara to get on while he and Jerome waited for the next one to come down. Trey and Jerome were talking when Trey remembered he left his phone in his car and told Jerome to hold the elevator for him if he came before he returned. Walking to his car while rubbing his temples, Trey didn't notice the speeding car coming towards him until it was too late. By the time Jerome reached him, Trey was lying on the ground bleeding from his head. Out of nowhere two security guards showed up saying they called for help. When the EMS arrived Jerome went with Trey but told the guards to alert Trey's family. No one seemed to notice the car that hit him slammed into another car.

The family waited to see how Trey was doing in the emergency waiting room. Trenton was mad as hell and demanded answers from Jerome. Tanya tried to calm him down, but he wasn't listening. Before he left the courthouse, he told Carl who was there to testify for the prosecution, to get on his damn job and review the tapes to see who tried to kill his son. It didn't help that Chris was there with a devilish smirk on his face while they were being told about Trey's accident. Trenton wanted to knock him into another world, but knew the fool wasn't worth his time.

Jerome was on the other side of the emergency waiting room giving his statement, but he didn't know how much help he would be since he didn't see anything. Tanya had Malinda brought to the waiting room and saw the pain on her daughter-in-law's face before she could say anything to her.

"I know who was behind Trey's accident." Malinda said.

"Little girl, what the hell you mean you know who hit my son? You better start talking quick. This wasn't no damn accident. It was attempted murder." The mincing words from Trenton gave Malinda the chills.

"My Aunt Maria was here about two hours ago trying to get me to talk to my dad. She was upset because she said he told her he didn't want to see her any longer."

"What the hell does that has to do with what happened to Trey?" Trenton didn't care about the crap Malinda was having with her crazy aunt.

"Trent give the girl a chance to finish." Tanya was sometimes embarrassed about how rude and abrupt her husband could be.

"She started going on and on about how her life is going down the tubes and started talking about how Trey wasn't good enough for me. She said he was having an affair with Sonya and making a fool out of me. She even had the nerve to say it was too bad he didn't die when he was in the hospital the first time."

"Why in the hell didn't you let the family know this was happening? If my brother is seriously hurt, it's your fault." Tara had tears in her eyes and was giving Malinda the evil eyes.

"Tara, you can't blame the actions of that woman on Linda." Talia was so sick of her sister always taking Trey's side and making Malinda out to be the heavy in every situation. But in this situation, Tara might be right because Malinda should have told the family about her aunt's visit.

"I don't know why your no-loyalty worthless behind is taking up for her." Tara shouted at Talia.

"Ladies this is a hospital. Cut this foolishness out right now. I'm going to see if I can find out something about Trey." Tanya was again embarrassed by her family. Jerome asked Tara to go with him to get some air. Talia stayed with Trenton, Trevor, and Malinda while they waited for TJ to make it to the hospital. They didn't know what was keeping him. Talia called him over an hour ago and he said he would meet them at the hospital. The group patiently waited for news on Trey hoping that nothing else would go wrong.

Detective Carl Marshall was trying to work his way through the events that happened today. He arrived at the courthouse earlier expecting to testify about the events that happened on the day his goddaughter was murder, but instead he found himself reviewing a videotape of the murder suspect in Trey Taylor's car accident. The driver didn't get very far because after the car hit Trey it collided into another car and the security guards was able to apprehend the suspect. While all of this was going on, two uniformed officers informed him about a call received from Trenton Taylor regarding Maria Dixon's rampage at the hospital.

Detective Marshall had to go to the hospital to question Maria but wasn't looking forward to running into the Taylor family. He couldn't say which one would be the worst the dad or the baby sister. He knew the family would be out for blood and expected him to do the collecting. He felt like he was letting his best friend down because he most definitely believed Trey was being framed as he thought from the beginning, but he had to go with the evidence. Chris was beginning to become unglued, and the more he tried to convince him they will get to the bottom of who murdered Sonya, the more erratic Chris' behavior became.

He was so glad he was approached by a doctor about fifteen minutes after arriving at the hospital getting permission to question Maria. Carl had a feeling this was going to be a long day and a not so pleasant one at that. After his questioning of Maria, he would have to touch base with the Taylor family. That was something he wasn't looking forward to doing. Opening the door to Maria's room Carl took a moment to look at the bruising on her face and the bandage on her left hand.

"Ms. Dixon, I'm Detective Marshall with the Chicago Police Department homicide unit. I need to ask you a few questions about the events of today."

"I don't have anything to say to you, Detective Marshall." Maria responded.

"What can you tell me about your injuries?" Carl continued ignoring Maria's response.

"What can you tell me about that no good ass Trey Taylor? Is that bastard dead?" Maria replied.

"What are you talking about, Ms. Dixon?" The vicious look that came on Maria's face made it clear to Carl that Maria was certifiable.

"You know damn well what I'm talking about. If you had done your job right and put that murdering bastard in prison where he belonged none of this would have happened."

"What does that have to do with the events of the today, Ms. Dixon?"

"It means that since you and your sorry ass department didn't take care of him the job was left to me."

"When you say him would you mind telling me the name of the person you're referring to?" Carl needed Maria to be crystal clear.

"Trey no good ass Taylor. That's whom I'm referring to."

"Could you please tell me what happened?"

"What happened is that man has taken everything that was important to me away. He and his high and mighty family think they're untouchable, but I guess after this morning they can see I can do more than reach out and touch."

"What do you mean by that statement, Ms. Dixon?"

"It means that I'm sick and tired of getting the crumbs off peoples table. I had the opportunity to finally be with the man I loved most of my adult life then he had to go and mess that up on top of taking my niece away from me."

"You still haven't told me about what happened this morning."

"I came to the hospital to visit my niece, Mindy to discuss some family issues, and she had her nose up in the air and wouldn't listen to anything I had to say. Then she started to go on and on about that sorry ass husband of hers, and said she wasn't going to lift a finger to help me with the issue I came to see her about. Things became a little heated and at that moment I knew I had to take care of him myself before he did any more damage to my life and my niece's life."

"How did you plan to take care of Trey, Ms. Dixon?"

"Well, my intentions were to go talk to him to see if he would help me with Mindy, but when I saw him laughing and joking with his family I saw red. He's on trial for murder and had the nerve to be enjoying time with his family and I'd just lost everything. I saw him break away from the family and head back towards his car and that was my opportunity to do what I had a feeling the courts wouldn't do."

"What did you do, Ms. Dixon?"

"I ran his ass down like the mangy dog that he is." Maria confessed.

"Ms. Dixon you're under arrest for the attempted murder of Trey Taylor. You have the right to remain silent. If you give up that right anything you say could be held against you. You have a right to an attorney. If you can't afford an attorney one will be appointed to you? Do you understand these rights as they have been stated to you, Ms. Dixon?"

"Yes. Now get out and leave me the hell alone." Carl cuffed Maria's right hand to the bed and told her an uniformed officer would be posted at her door before he left.

## Chapter Twenty-Nine

The noises in the background became louder. It seemed the people shouting at each other didn't care that he had awaken even though everything was a blur. Trying to focus and figure out where he was and what was going on, he finally recognized a voice that he's been trying to get out of his life for a long time, Sonya. Keeping his eyes closed so they wouldn't notice he had awakened, Trey tried to place some of the other voices. All the voices seemed familiar, but with his head hurting so badly and with everyone shouting it was hard to make out what was going on. Sonya seemed to be the most upset out of the group. Concentrating Trey was able to understand what she was yelling to the others.

*"How come you people didn't listen and follow the plan like we talked about so many times?" Trey didn't have to see Sonya's face to know she was frowning.*

*"Maybe because everyone wants to be the chief. This plan was devised down to the letter. If everyone had carryout their part things would have flowed better." This time it was no mistaken that voice. It was Chris Young.*

*"We don't have time to argue. Let's get this over with before he wakes up. The last thing we need is to drug him again and for it to show up in his system." That was Maria and her tone was so hateful there was no mistake she was ready to get the show on the road.*

*"Everything is all set. You two get out of here and make sure you leave through the secret panel. Remember no talking to anyone and be ready to put on the acting of your lives when the shit hits the fan." Trey could hear Mr. Chris sobbing as he peeked to see that he was now hugging Sonya. Once Maria gave Sonya a hug she and Mr. Chris headed towards the back of the condo.*

*The main voice that Trey was still finding it hard to recognize was telling Sonya how much he loved her. Giving her a passionate kiss, the pair parted then for some reason Sonya keeled down until she was on her knees. Everything else happened so quickly. Trey saw a gun in the man's hand. Trying to get up, Trey was hit over the head again which caused everything to go almost black. Trey felt the man standing over him and roughly grabbed Trey's left hand. Feeling the gloved hand putting the gun into his hand, Trey heard the gun going off and everything else went blank.*

The nurses near the ICU heard the yelling coming from Trey's room. They were worried about him because he'd been so restless. The family was visiting the baby because of the medication Trey was on the doctors told them it will be hours before he was conscious. When the nurses rushed into the room, they saw Trey thrashing around in the bed yelling no over and over. They did their best to restrain him and were glad when the doctor finally arrived. He told one of the nurses to contact his family while he gave Trey a mild sedative to calm him down. It only took a few minutes for this to work. By the time the doctor checked his vitals Trey's family was there.

"Tanya, I know you and Talia know the drill. I'm sorry to have to tell you that I had to put restraints on Trey." The doctor felt he had to do this for Trey's safety, so he wouldn't disturb his sutures.

"What the hell are you talking about restraining my son?" Trenton didn't care the doctor was mainly addressing his wife and daughter he wanted to know why the doctor was doing this crazy shit to his son.

"Calm down, Trent. This is normal procedure to protect the patient from rupturing sutures after surgery." Tanya wished her husband would listen to the complete explanation before he flew off the handle.

"The nurses said that Trey was yelling to the top of his lungs, and they couldn't calm him down. When I arrived in the room he was thrashing in his bed, so I had to give him a mild sedative and ordered the restraints." The doctor's pager went off, so he had to leave the family.

"When is all of this going to stop? Trey is living in constant fear of sleeping because of these bad dreams." Malinda was sobbing, and Talia went over to console her.

"Why didn't you let us know that Trey was having these kinds of problems?" Trenton was sick and tired of Malinda keeping things from them.

"Dad, Linda didn't do anything wrong. Trey didn't want the family to know he was having a few issues with everything else going on in the family. He stayed with me for a little while because he didn't want to bother the rest of the family." Trevor tried to take some of the heat off his sister-in-law.

"That's not good enough. How are we supposed to help him if we don't know what's going on in his life?" Trenton refused to let this go until he saw Chief Marshall and decided he had a bigger fish to fry.

"I hope you got that crazy ass woman behind bars?" Trenton said.

"Hello to you too, Trenton. To answer your question yes Maria Dixon has been arrested for hitting Trey. She's here at the hospital right now because of the injuries she suffered during the accident." Carl was used to Trenton's abrupt behavior.

"Well that's good news. About time your office is doing their job. Now all you need to do is find out who murdered Sonya."

"We're working on that. How is Trey doing?" Carl wanted to change the subject until he could confirm the information he just received. He could see a nurse approaching them.

"Mr. Taylor your son is asking to see you guys." The family including Chief Marshall entered Trey's room. Tanya knew all of them shouldn't be in there at one time, but all of them were worried about Trey. When Trey noticed that Carl was with them, he asked him to come closer to the bed.

"I know who framed me. It was Mr. Chris, my wife's Aunt Maria, and Judge Winston." The people in the room were shocked by the last name Trey gave, but not the Chief.

"I take it you've gotten your memory back." Carl asked.

"Most of it, I remembered everyone in the room arguing and after Mr. Chris and Maria left the condo the Judge kissed Sonya and she got down on her knees. As he approached me, I saw he had a gun in his hand. I tried to get away, but the drugs they gave me wouldn't allow me to move fast enough."

"They better hope I don't get my hands on them." Trenton said.

"I heard them talking about giving me something that was untraceable. Anyway, when I realized that Judge Winston was about to put the gun in my hand, I tried to resist he hit me with the butt of the gun. With his gloved hands he put the gun in my left-hand right before I passed out I heard the shots"

"Since drugs were found in your system, I guess that plan didn't work out well for them." Tara said.

"Trey, I wanted to wait until I've gotten confirmation, but it seemed that Ms. Dixon wasn't going to go down alone, so she told the prosecutor the whole story to try to cut a deal. She may have gotten it if she wasn't arrested for hitting you." Carl was in so much pain because his best friend had lost touch with reality without him being the wiser.

"What's the whole story, Chief Marshall?" Tara wanted to know all the gory details.

"The plan was devised by Judge Winston with at first only Chris and Sonya's involvement. Chris let some of the plan slip to Maria whom he was having an affair with for some time."

"Good Lord, Sharon is going to be devastated." Tanya was worried about how her friend would cope when all of this comes to light.

"Ms. Dixon wanted Trey to pay for taking Malinda away and for her rocky relationship with Mr. Roberts. Since Malinda and her siblings were giving Mr. Roberts a hard time about the relationship he began to pull away. That's when she latched onto Chris Young. Their dislike for Trey provided them with a common goal. When they were almost done with the planning Chris, Maria, and Sonya were pissed when Judge Winston brought in his son Malcolm and his girlfriend Joanna. The judge felt they needed additional help in making it look like Trey and Sonya was having an affair." Carl explained.

"So, you're saying all the suspects are in custody now?" Trevor was so glad this ordeal was over.

"Everyone except for Malcolm Winston. The other suspects were arrested at work, but we haven't been able to track down Malcolm." Carl knew there would be more questions, but the nurse came into the room and said they had to leave because only two could be in there at a time. Trenton and Trevor stayed while the others went to meet in a private room the nurse escorted them to. They were in the room about ten minutes when the Chief excused himself saying that Malcolm had been arrested.

"I can't believe these people would go through so much trouble to get rid of Trey." Tara was amazed at the elaborate plan these criminals set into play. Trenton and Trevor came in saying Trey was sleeping.

"I knew Malcolm wanted Linda back, but I didn't think he would go this far." Talia said. She knew Tara was going to have a smart comment.

"Well if she had shut him down like Trey tried to do with Sonya's crazy behind maybe they wouldn't have taken things this far and Trey wouldn't be in the hospital." Tara was rolling her eyes at Malinda.

"Tara this isn't my fault. I haven't been with Mal for years. He wasn't harassing me like Sonya was harassing Trey, so I wasn't aware there was a problem." Malinda explained.

"Cut it out, Tara. Linda maybe you should go check on the baby. If we hear anything about Trey or the case, we'll send someone to get you." Tanya wanted to keep the two ladies apart because she knew her youngest daughter had a knack for not letting things go.

"Ok, but make sure you guys let me know about any changes." Malinda was about to leave when Talia said she will go with her.

After the ladies left the room, Tara asked while pouting, "Mom why do you always take Linda's side?"

"I don't always take her side, Tara. It's just you don't leave room for anyone's opinion but yours at times. Malinda is going through a lot with the baby, Trey, and her dad."

"I just hope she's a better mom than she is a wife." Tara mumbled.

"Tara didn't your mom say cut it out. We need to be focusing on getting the state to drop their case against your brother." The room got quiet after Trenton made that statement as TJ walked into the room. "Where have you been all morning?"

"Out working this case. I've been doing it since we met at your house. I knew Trey wouldn't trust me to help, so I've been helping from behind the scene. I was instrumental in bringing in all the suspects including Malcolm." Tanya got up from her seat next to her husband and gave TJ a big hug followed by Trevor. Trenton and Jerome did the same, but Tara didn't make a move, so TJ went over to her seat and started tickling her. At first, she wouldn't budge and then decided to give her brother a hug. They all decided to go over to the big house since it would be a while before they'll be able to see Trey.

## Epilogue

Family and friends gathered to celebrate Thanksgiving dinner at Trenton and Tanya's. The Taylor family had a lot to be thankful for this year starting with the state dropping the case against Trey. Joanna Dawson was the only one that didn't receive any prison time for her part in Trey's framing because she was able to prove that she was forced into cooperating with the rest of the bunch. Judge Winston found out she had a misdemeanor she didn't put on her bank application. Since she was taking care of her two sisters and sick mom, she couldn't afford to lose her job or the new promotion she recently received. She was also scared to death of Malcolm. With all their connections she knew father and son had her just where they needed her to execute their plan. Malcolm had gotten physically violent with her on the few occasions when she tried to back out of what they wanted her to do.

Judge Winston was in love with Sonya. He was willing to do anything to make her happy. Sonya refused any treatment and had planned to kill herself before the group came up with this plan that made her happy for a while because she would be able to take Trey down with her. Malcolm was stupid enough to think that if Trey was out of the picture, he could get Malinda back. Sonya made them promise not to kill Trey because he wouldn't suffer like she had over the years chasing him. Her dad was so messed up when he found out her diagnosis, he lost touch with reality and was a willing participant. All of Sonya's problems became Trey's fault in her dad's mind even her Cancer, so his resentment grew stronger with each day that passed. He even had problems with his wife because she didn't support their daughter enough. He was tired of hearing Sharon saying Sonya needed professional help and for taking Trey's side when he filed that restraining order against Sonya.

They all were sentence to life in prison with extra charges against Maria hitting Trey. The great news the Taylor's celebrated just a week ago was when Tyrell Ashton Taylor was released from the hospital. It was hard keeping the family away during the first few days. Ty was still small, but the joy he brought to the family was unimaginable. Now sitting around the Taylor's huge dinner table Trey wanted to make an announcement.

"Family and friends, we don't know how to thank all of you for your love and support during the most trying times in our life, my murder case and Tyrell's early birth. Linda and I wouldn't have been able to make it without your support. We love and appreciate all of you."

Linda stood after Trey finished speaking. "We would like to give a special thanks to TJ for the work he performed on Trey's behalf. Now, what we all need to do in put all of this behind us and enjoy what we have to look forward to especially this Sunday when we celebrate Ty's christening." Malinda sat down as Tanya took the floor.

"This may not be the time to bring this up, but I would like to let Sharon know how proud I am of her for moving on with her life after the tragedies she's suffered this year. I know it was hard for her to let go of her daughter in such a violent way and the husband whose meltdown became a public disgrace. Now that she's a single woman again, for now because I plan on having her social life booked to the next century." Everyone in the room had to laugh at Tanya's speech because even though it was said in jest they all knew that would be her next full time job finding her friend a new mate.

"I would like to have the last say before you all eat all my damn food up. Life will bring many challenges but having the support of family and friends will always trump negative actions and thoughts. My youngest son almost lost his freedom because of hateful people who weren't satisfied with their lives. Now as he and his wife celebrate the next generation with Tyrell and the great selection of godparents for their son my daughter Talia and Trey's best friend Jerome let us be thankful that all of our prayers have been answered. To life, love, family, and friendship may we all be as happy in the future as we are today." After the toast the eating began.

# Dark Revenge: The Trey Taylor Story
## Discussion Questions

1) Do you think Trey was guilty of Sonya's murder with all the evidence stacked against him?

2) Do you feel Chief Marshall would be able to be objective since he's had a strained relationship with Trey and was the best friend of Chris and Sonya's godfather?

3) Do you think Trey did all he could to cut his ties to Sonya?

4) Was it unfair the way the family treated Talia and TJ because they weren't sure if Trey was guilty?

5) Why do you believe Trey was having problems remembering what happened that day?

6) Do you think Talia was wrong for asking Trey if he was having an affair with Sonya?

7) Have you ever known anyone that was obsessed with someone as bad as Sonya was with Trey?

8) What do you think about Trenton and his actions handling Trey's case, family members, and friends?

9) Do you feel Corey Sr. and Maria were responsible for Malinda's emergency C-Section?

10) Why do you think Sharon wasn't aware of what her husband was up to?

11) Do you think Malinda and her siblings were justified in their feelings regarding their dad's relationship with their aunt?

12) Do you feel that Joanna should have been charged for her part in framing Trey?

Dear Reader,

I hope you enjoyed reading the rewrite of **Dark Revenge: The Trey Taylor Story.** This book was first published in March 2017. The decision behind revamping this book was to relaunch the first book in this three-book series. This step was taken in anticipation of enhancing marketing strategies in hopes of generating renewed interest in the series. I like to keep my readers entertained by writing something that is satisfying and inspirational.

It would be greatly appreciated if you would consider writing a review of this title on Amazon, Barnes & Noble, and/or author's website dianacarterwriter.com in the Comments section under Contact Us (located under the More tab). You can also write a review in the same locations about any of my other titles you may have read. When you visit my website, you will learn more about other titles, upcoming events, publishing services offered, and more.

God's blessings,

Diana Carter

You can find me on the web:

Website: www.dianacarterwriter.com
Amazon Author Page: www.amazon.com/author/diana.carter
Goodreads: www.Goodreads.com/dianacarter

## Author's Information

Diana Carter started her writing career after taking a personality test many years ago and disagreeing with the results. After talking to the administrator of that test, Diana was encouraged to submit the book she had written for publication. Born was the first book in the four-book *Broken Promises* series. *Broken Promises: Shattered Dreams* was published on April 10, 2014. This book has been rewritten along with books two and three in the series.

The second book, *Broken Promises: When Shattered Dreams Become Reality* was published the following year on April 15, 2015. The rewrite of this book is expected to be release later this year. The third book in the series *Broken Promises: Shattered Dreams The Final Chapter* was published on June 27, 2016. The rewrite of this book will also be published later this year. All three rewritten books will be published by Let's Do This Publishing, LLC (LDTP). This publishing company was founded by the Diana in July 2017. The last book in this series *In The Name of Justice: The Erica Blackstone Chronicles* was published on December 8, 2017, by LDTP.

In between the third and fourth books in the *Broken Promises* series, this rewritten book *Dark Revenge: The Trey Taylor Story* was first published on March 30, 2017. The four-book *The Sister Factor* series and its Spin-Off *Never a Dull Moment: The Nick Jr. Story* were all published in 2018, along with the sequel to *Dark Revenge, When Time Runs Out: Tara's Quest for Vengeance* and *The Candidate: The Race to the Top.* On January 4, 2019 *Dark Revenge: TJ The Forgotten Brother* was published. *Unbreakable: When Two Hearts Become One* was published on March 23, 2019. This is the first romance book written by the author. *The Making of a Legend: Neek's Rise to Fame* was published on August 13, 2019. The author's latest book was published on December 27, 2019, *Unbreakable Deux.* This is the sequel to *Unbreakable: When Two Hearts Become One.*

Diana has a passion for writing fiction stories that will not only entertain her readers but also have a lasting impact. She loves to write and looks forward to continuing for many years to come. When she takes a break from writing, she likes to spend time with her children and grandchildren, bowl, read, and tutoring disadvantaged adults.

You can find additional information on Diana's website at www.dianacarterwriter.com or if you like to personally reach her do so via email at diana.carter44@gmail.com.

CPSIA information can be obtained
at www.ICGtesting.com
Printed in the USA
BVHW031952100520
579476BV00001B/12